SMALL SCALE INDUSTRY

SMALL SCALE INDUSTRY

By

Dr. M. Lakshmi Narasaiah
M.A., Ph.D.

&

Dr. B. Deevena Margaret
M.A., Ph.D.

Department of Economics
Sri Krishnadevaraya University
Anantapur – 515 003
(Andhra Pradesh)

DISCOVERY
PUBLISHING HOUSE

First Published - 1999

Reprinted - 2025

ISBN: 978-81-7141-469-7

Small Scale Industry

Published by:

DISCOVERY PUBLISHING HOUSE
4383/4B, Ansari Road, Darya Ganj
New Delhi-110 002 (India)
Phone: +91-11-23279245, 23253475; 43596065
E-mail: discoverybooksindia@gmail.com
orderdphbooks@gmail.com
web: www.discoverypublishinggroup.com

Printed at:
Infinity Imaging Systems
Delhi

Preface

The Small-Scale Industry (SSI) has been recognised as one of the most appropriate means of developing the industrial economy of backward countries. Small-Scale Industries facilitate the tapping of resources which otherwise would remain unused. These resources include entrepreneurship, capital, labour and raw materials. They can mobilise rural savings which may otherwise remain idle or may be spent on luxuries or channelled into non-productive ventures.

They are fairly labour-intensive. Small-Scale industries create employment opportunities at a relatively low capital cost. In India, there is a basic problem of absorbing the surplus manpower in non-agricultural jobs and providing additional employment opportunities for the growing population.

Small-Scale Industries contribute significantly to the straightening of the industrial structure. It serves as seed-beds of entrepreneurship. They serve the developing economy not only by their output of goods but also by functioning as a nursery of entrepreneurial and managerial talent. This role of SSIs is of decisive importance in any economy.

Such industries lead to the creation of employment opportunities as a dispersed basis not only in large cities and towns but also in smaller towns and far-flung regions. The establishment of SSIs would, therefore, make it possible to reverse the current trend of the migration of the people from rural to urban areas.

The development of small-scale sector has been important in India because the small-scale unit requires less capital outlay and at the same time, it provides more employment than the large scale sector. A small scale unit does not require highly sophisticated technology. It can, therefore, be usual in backward areas where the people are yet to be trained to meet the challenge of sophisticated technology.

Soon after independence, our national leaders recognised the role of small-scale sector in the development of the economy of India and laid a solid foundation for its accelerated development through active policy support and creation of an institutional frame work. The Industrial Policy Resolutions of the Government of India, from 1948 to 1991 visualised integrated growth of both the large and small-scale sectors and recognised the social and economic contribution of small-scale sector. These Industrial Policy Resolutions state that the Government of India would stress the role of cottage and village and SSIs in the development of the national economy. The policy further envisages that the decentralised sector should acquire sufficient vitality to be self-supporting and its development be integrated with that of the large scale industry.

Authors

Contents

1

Introduction

Statement of the Problem

The Small-Scale Industry has been recognised as one of the most appropriate means of developing the industrial economy of backward countries. Small-Scale Industries facilitate the tapping of resource which otherwise would remain unused. These resources included entrepreneurship, capital, labour and raw materials. They can mobilize rural savings which may otherwise remain idle or may be spent on luxuries or channelled into non productive ventures.

They are fairly labour intensive, Small-Scale Industries which create employment opportunities at a relatively low capital cost. In India, there is a basic problem of absorbing the surplus manpower in non-agriculture jobs and providing additional employment opportunities for the growing population.

Small-Scale Industries contribute significantly to the strengthening of the industrial structure. Small-Scale Industries serve as seed-beds of entrepreneurship. They serve the developing economy not only by their output of goods but also by functioning as a nursery of entrepreneurial and managerial talent. This role of Small-Scale Industries is of decisive importance in any economy.

Such industries lead to the creation of employment opportunities as a dispersed basis not only in large cities and towns but also in smaller towns and far-flung regions. The establishment of Small-Scale Industries would therefore made it possible to reverse the current trend of the migration of the people from rural to urban areas.

The development of Small-Scale Sector has been importance in India because the Small-Scale Unit requires less capital outlay and at the same time, it provides more employment than the large-scale sector. A Small-Scale Unit does not require highly sophisticated technology. It can therefore, be useful in backward areas where the people have yet to be trained to meet the challenge of sophisticated technology.

Soon after independence our national leaders recognised the role of Small-Scale Sector in the development of the economy of India and laid a solid foundation for its accelerated development through active policy support and creation of an institutional frame work. The Industrial Policy Resolutions of the Government of India, from 1948 to 1991 visualized integrated growth of the both the large and Small-Scale Sectors and recognised the social and economic contribution of Small-Scale Sector. These Industrial Policy Resolutions states that the Government of India would stress the role of cottage and village and Small-Scale Industries in the development of the national economy. The policy further envisaged that the decentralised sector should acquire sufficient vitality to be self supporting and its development be integrated with that of the large-scale industry.

Anantapur District is located in the Southern part of Andhra Pradesh. It is an economically backward district. The main livelihood of the people is agriculture. For the past several decades, there has been failure of rains in the region. As there is no prospects of agriculture in this district, people have stated move to neighboring districts, particularly to Karnataka area to ekeout their livelihood.,

In view of this prevailing situation, the unemployed educated youths are evincing interest to establish Small-Scale Industries with the help and assistance of Schedule Banks, State Finance Corporations etc. The Government of Andhra Pradesh has initiated several industrial programmes to make the State on par with other industrially developed states. As a part of its policy, the Government of Andhra Pradesh has announced several incentives to entrepreneurs who want to start Small-Scale Industrial units. The establishment of Small-Scale Industrial units is best suited to this district in view of the availability of raw materials from agriculture and mineral based and other industries. The establishment of Small-Scale Industries will be boon to the people of Anantapur District to lift the people above poverty line. The Small-Scale Industries, inspite of encouraging entrepreneurs, generates employment opportunities to the needy. The pivotal role of District Industries centre in advising the enthusiastic entrepreneurs to move forward to achieve their goal is highly commendable.

The burning problem facing the Government is how to solve unemployment. As we know, the Government alone cannot start or declar war against unemployment, the unemployed educated youths should take positive interest in establishing Small-Scale Industries in support of Governmental efforts, to solve this unemployment problem.

For establishing Small-Scale Industries, the know-how of capital structure, employment generation, locating the industrial belt and other aspects of industrial establishment are a must for any prospective entrepreneurs. There seems to be no other go except establishing Small-Scale Industries where ever feasible solve the problem of Unemployment. Such an attempt would necessarily provide the opportunity for the optimum utilisation of local resources to serve the local needs.

The Large-Scale Industry is urban based. It has resulted in the neglect of agriculture and industry in the Rural areas. The establishment of Small-Scale Industries can serve as an effective means of reducing the prevailing imbalances. It helps in accelerating process of overall development of the State.

Select Review of the Literature

Some studies have been undertaken on various programmes and incentives to small industries promotional activities of DICS and problems associated with the implementation of the promotional institutions and the problems faced by the entrepreneurs. SIET (1972)[1] in its study on Hire-purchase has observed that the growth in the number of units and the expansion of capital intensity alone may not create the necessary impetus to the growth unless considerable productivity changes have also been effected through fuller capacity utilisation. Most of the units utilising full-capacity have been either big export-oriented industries or local-need-based activities. The reasons for this under utilisation were mostly insufficient demand for inadequate financial resources for working capital. In a study a spatial diversification of manufacturing industries in Uttar Pradesh, Papola (1979)[2], while furnishing evidence of a continued spatial concentration has noted a decline in the share of factory employment in five most industrialised districts from 57 per cent in 1960 to 55 per cent in 1975 and also in 10 industrially least developed areas from 1.10 per cent to 0.56 per cent. He has concluded that there is a need for a small degree of dispersal of manufacturing activity in favour of backward areas with some degree of industrialisation. Malgawekar (1973)[3], in his study of problems of small industry in Andhra Pradesh has found the lack of infrastructure as a general problems. The industrial estates alone cannot overcome the locational disadvantages. The infrastructural facilities were either very weak or non-existent in rural areas. In Urban areas, with necessary industrial climate and infrastructure facilities, the growth of industries was relatively faster. The scarcity of indigenous raw materials has been a serious bottleneck. Scarce raw materials supplied through quotas were not sufficient to meet the demands of the units. There were delays in the disbursement of the loans due to the existence of procedural delays and instance of tangible securities.

The development of Small Industry also depends on the size of market which in turn depends partly on the efficiency of the size of market which in turn depends partly on the efficiency of the distribution of machinery. It is observed that there was a time lag between sales and realisation of sale proceeds and this affected production of the enterprise. This study has also found that the incentives provided by the state and the centre were not within the reach of all the entrepreneurs in rural areas.

Andhra Pradesh Industrial Technical Consultancy Organisation (A.P.I.T.C.O) and Kerala Industrial Technical Consultancy Organisation (K.I.T.C.O.) 1980[4] conducted a study of the various problems faced by the industries in three states viz., Kerala, Karnataka and Andhra Pradesh. The study revealed that the serious problem faced by the units was the inadequacy of working capital. 69 per cent of units in Kerala, 44 per cent of units in Karnataka and 52 per cent of units in Andhra Pradesh were facing the same problem. The next serious problem was marketing as 30 per cent of the units of Kerala felt it as another setback. Non-availability of raw materials has affected the productivity of several units in all the states especially, in industry groups such as metal-products in Kerala, Chemicals, Rubber and Plastics and metal products in Karnataka, machinery and parts, metal products and chemicals in Andhra Pradesh. It was observed, that the delay in getting timely finance also hampered the productivity of the units and this led to high cost of production, as observed in a few cases, in all the states.

Sarma (1982)[5] who made a study on growth and problems of Small-Scale Sector in Andhra Pradesh, has observed that the backward districts of the State improved their relative positions in terms of units employment and capital during 1966-75. Majority of the small units are confronted with the problems of raw materials and finance.

Sekhar (1983)[6] in his study has observed that the location policies were successful in narrowing the disparities of industrial location in different states. The value added and employment were more equally distributed among the states during 1960 and 1975 as measured by the Theils inequality and the Harschman Hirfindhal's indices. He also examined intra-regional distribution of industry by comparing the degree of concentration of industrial employment in 1961 and 1971 by grouping cities by size and arrived at the conclusion that, for India as a whole, the degree of concentration of employment in household industry has declined substantially between 1961 and 1971. However, the non-house hold industry maintained its level of concentration during the period.

Rajula Devi (1984)[7] in her study made on the evaluation of Rural industries Project Programme found the following serious deficiencies (i) Some part of the assistance was provided to relatively larger amongst small-scale units, (ii) Assistance was diverted to towns which were excluded from the preview of the scheme (iii) Rural artisans did not receive adequate credit. Indian Institute of Management (1988)[8] in its study conducted on "Evaluation of

DIC programme in Andhra Pradesh observed that the General Manager, DIC, as Secretary to the single window committee is expected to hasten up the processing of entrepreneurial cases and thus help the minimisation of delay. Single Window Committee just recommends and requests for speeder action and the DIC have no powers to hasten up and clean up such delayed cases. Several entrepreneurs in every DIC have been annoyed to find their cases long pending with developmental agencies and local bodies due to indifferent attitude and lack of emphathetic understanding of entrepreneurial problems. With regard to the activities like term-loan assistance, working capital assistance, capital subsidy, land and factory shed, many entrepreneurs seemed to have received the requisite help from DIC. In these activities, DICs have mostly recommending powers. For raw materials and other information DIC's seem to be playing a very small role.

DICs have been functioning for over a decade since their inception. The above studies have tried to indicate certain deficiencies of various schemes including District Industries centres but they have not evaluated the performance of DIC at a regional level. Hence, it is time to undertake an evaluative study which is area-specific since India is a vast country with varied socio-economic conditions.

Bhagavati Committee[9] opposes fast introduction of mechanisation designed to replace human labour but, at the same time, recommends introduction of sophisticate technology in certain areas. The Committee recommends reduction to the maximum extent possible in the installed capacity in various industries in order to generate employment in the industrial field. The committee virtually favours creation of employment at any cost without going into the economics of the scheme.

In a study on rural industrialisation in India Bepin Behari[10] examined the problems, possibilities and perspectives of rural industrialisation and discussed the crisis in Indian villages and the need for the new strategy of rural industrialisation and the provision of fuller employment in rural and small-scale industries and technologies. He traced out agricultural development encouragement to village and small-scale industries and general awareness for incorporating appropriate technologies as principal sources of impetus to the programme of technological transformation in rural India. Further he reviewed various measures taken by the Government towards rural industrialisation, local industrial growth, agro based industries, mini-rural cement plants, utilisation of annual waste and harnessing of natural power.

K.V. Bhanuja[11], has suggested that appropriate technology should be developed to promote the rural small industries, N.V. Ratnam[12] opines that infrastructure development for industrialisation in the rural areas and investment in basic services designed to realise the full potential of the human resources in the rural areas should receive a high priority.

Gunnar Myrdal[13] has recommended the adoption of a strategy based on predominantly labour intensive techniques for creating capital and production. The line of approach has been followed up by Sen[14] Johnson[15], Vinod Vyasulu[16] and Raj Krishna[17] suggesting the need for the adoption of an employment-oriented strategy of industrialisation to absorb the rural !abour force.

Tin Bergen[18] opines that strategy of industrialisation should lay emphasis on labour intensive industries which will create more employment and maximise income. He suggests the adoption of labour-intensive but reasonable efficient techniques. Gautam Mathur[19] opines that the appropriate techniques in the consumption-goods sector will be of a low degree of mechanisation creating incidentally a lot of employment per unit of investment of scarce capital. Dr. Wu, Jageh[20] in his study pointed out that both the capital output ratio and wage-capital ratio show an inverse relationship with capital intensity. He recommends the setting up of SSI in countries having large unemployment. A.C. Minocha[21] has suggested that the strategy of employment-oriented industrialisation should aim at the development of SSI in rural areas. K.M. Rastogi[22], in his study suggests that the SSI should make use of the indigenous resources in an optimal manner. UNIDO's[23] study indicates that the small enterprises with low-level of investment per worker tend to achieve a higher productivity of capital.

The Committee[24] on the village and SSI in its report has stressed that the setting up of SSI will provide employment to the people in rural areas.

K.M. Rostagi[25] has also made a case study of Madhya Pradesh which he calls a Unique case of growing unemployment and poverty amidst plenty. He is in favour of only Small-Scale and village Industries which make optimum use of indigenous resources and techniques. According to him, there are hundreds of items which can be produced in rural and Small-Scale Industrial units more economically than in a large sector.

Bhagavati[26] Committee opposes fast introduction of mechanisation designed to replace human labour but, at the same time recommends introduction of sophisticated technology in certain select areas. The Committee recommends reduction to the maximum extent possible in the installed-capacity in various industries in order to generate employment in the industrial field. The Committee virtually favour creation of employment at any cost without going into economics of the scheme.

The Present Study

In a vast country like India with varied resource-base and socio economic conditions, macro level studies may not throw much light as the problems of all regions thus more micro level studies for each region are necessary for understanding the prospects and problems of small-scale industrial units in different regions of our country. The present study conducted in Anantapur District, one of the drought prone and backward district of Andhra Pradesh is a modest attempt in this direction, which throws much light on the problems and prospects of small-scale industrial units at the district level.

Objectives

The main objectives of the present study are

1. To analyse the structural characteristics of the capital of the small-scale industrial units.
2. To examine the employment, capital structure and out put in small-scale industrial units.
3. To identify the operational problems and prospects of small-scale industrial units.

Hypothesis

1. There is no variation among sample units with regard to total output and there is no relationship between capital and output.

2. The employment and capital in various categories of sample units in not significant and there is no significant relation between employment and capital.

Methodology

Data Base

Survey method has been adopted for this study, Data for the study have been collected from both primary and secondary sources. Secondary sources include Census Reports, Plan Documents of Central and State Governments, Financial Institutions, District Industries Centre and Statistical Abstracts of India and Andhra Pradesh. Primary data have been collected from sample small-scale industrial units through a schedule constructed for the purpose.

Sample Design

In the case of large, medium and small-scale industries, adequate data are available with the official and non-official agencies. Since the number of units are too large to carry out a Census enumeration. There are 477 small-scale units in the study area. But in the case of small-scale industries, simple random sampling method has been used for the present study. The selected units operating in Anantapur District represent seven industrial categories of small-scale industries. Totally 95 sample units in all the seven categories, are selected for the study. Thus the sample size for the study is 95 units as detailed in Table 1.1.

Table 1.1 : Category-wise Distribution of Sample Units

Sl. No.	*Category of Industry*	*Total No. of Units Available*	*Sample Units 20%*
1.	Agro-based Industries	120	23
2.	Engineering Industries	124	24
3.	Forest based Industries	29	7
4.	Textile Based Industries	35	8
5.	Mineral Industries	20	4
6.	Chemical Based Industries	34	7
7.	Miscellaneous Industries	115	22
	Total	477	95

Tools of Analysis

In addition to usual statistical measures such as ratios, percentages, and averages, analyses are employed at appropriate contexts in the study. And also various statistical tools are used in the study to analyse the data as follows:

a) *Correlation Co-efficient*

In order to study the relationship between Fixed Capital employment and output, of small-scale industrial units correlation co-efficient of the following form has been employed

$$r = \frac{\frac{\Sigma xy - \Sigma x - \Sigma y}{n}}{\sqrt{\left[\Sigma x^2 - \frac{(\Sigma x^2)}{n}\right]}\sqrt{\left[\Sigma y^2 - \frac{(\Sigma y^2)}{n}\right]}}$$

Where r = Co-efficient of Correlation

x = Deviation of X from its mean i.e., $x-\bar{x}$

y = Deviation of Y from its mean i.e., $y-\bar{y}$

Scale Product Method

In order to examine the intensity of the problems of sample units scale product method of the following form has been employed

$$\text{Scale product value} = \frac{r_1 s_1 + r_2 s_2 + r_3 s_3}{n}$$

$$= \frac{r_1 s_1 + r_2 s_2 + r_3 s_3}{n}$$

Where r_1 = The percentage of Total assigned the Weight s_1

r_2 = The percentage of total Assigned the Weight s_2

r_3 = The percentage of total assigned the Weight s_3

Analysis of Variance

In order to study the variation in capital invested and production between units and between categories analysis of variance (ANOVA) of the following form has been employed:

Source of Variation	*Sum of squares*	*Degrees of freedom*	*Mean square*	*F*
Between Samples (Columns)	SSC	K–1	MSC	
Within Samples	SSE	n–K	MSE	MSC/MSE
Total	SST	n–1		

SSC = Sum of squares between column means

SSE = Sum of squares within or for error

SST = Total sum of squares

MSC = Mean square between samples

MSE = Mean square within sampls

Again SST = $\Sigma x_1^2 + \Sigma x_2^2 + \Sigma x_3^2 \; .... \; \Sigma x_n^2 = T^2/N$

$$SSC = \frac{(\Sigma x_1)^2}{N_1} + \frac{(\Sigma x_2)^2}{N_2} + ... + \frac{(\Sigma x_n)^2}{N_v} = \frac{(T)^2}{N}$$

T^2/n = Correlation factor

T = The sum of all the items of various samples

N = Total number of Sample Units

SSE = SST – SSC

MSC = SSC/K–1, Where K = number of categories of units

MSE = SSE/n–k

Standard Deviation

The standard deviation measures the absolute dispersion variability of a distribution, the greater the amount of dispersion of variability, the greater the standard deviation (for the greater will be the magnitude of the deviations of the values from their mean. A small standard deviation means a high degree of uniformity of the observations as well as homogeneity of a series, a large standard deviation means just the opposite of assumed mean method

t–test

$$t = \frac{r\sqrt{n-2}}{\sqrt{1-r^2}} \qquad \sigma = \sqrt{\frac{1}{n}\Sigma x_i^2 - \bar{x}^2}$$

where,

n = Total number of units

r = Correlation co-efficient

Co-efficient of Variation

It is used in such problems where we went to compare the variability of two or more than two series that series or group for which the C.V. is greater is said to be more variable or conversely less consistent, less uniform, less stable or less homogenous

$$C.V. = \frac{\sigma}{\bar{x}} \times 100$$

Scope and Limitation of the Study

1. The study has covered only 95 small-scale industries located in Anantapur District.
2. Only seven categories of industries are considered for the study.
3. The focus of the study is category-wise rather than on area wise analysis.
4. Mainly concentrated on the capital structure, employment problems and prospects of sample units.

Due to these limitations, the conclusions arrived at in the present study may not be applicable to other parts of the country as India is a vast country with regional variations in research endowments entrepreneurial talents, infrastructural facilities and socio-economic conditions.

Plan of the Thesis

The present thesis is organised in seven chapters. The first chapter deals with the statement of the problem a study of select review of literature and objectives, hypothesis and methodology of the present study. The Second chapter consists of small-scale industries in India, policies, programmes and performance. The third chapter portrays the socio-economic features and industrial economy of Anantapur District. Fourth chapter provides the analysis of capital structure of small-scale industries. The relationship between employment and capital, capital and output has been presented in the fifth chapter. Sixth chapter presents the problems and prospects of the sample units. Summary of findings and conclusions form the Seventh Chapter.

References

1. Small Industries Extension Training (SIET). A study of National Small Industries Corporation is Hire purchase Scheme, Hyderabad SIET Institute, March, 1972.
2. People, T.S., Spatial Diversification of Manufacturing Industries in Uttar Pradesh, Lucknow, Giri Institute of Development Studies, 1979.
3. Malgawakar, P.D., "Problems of Small Industry, A study in Andhra Pradesh", Hyderabad, SIET, 1973.
4. Andhra Pradesh Industrial Technical Consultancy Organisation and Kerala Industries Technical Consultancy Organisation, "Survey of Industrial Estates in India, Semion Industrial Development of Backward Areas, sponsored by industrial Development Bank of India, May 7, 1980.
5. Sarma, R.K. Industrial Development of Andhra Pradesh. A Regional Analysis, Bombay, Himalaya Publishing House, 1982.
6. Sekhar, A., Uday, Industrial Location Policy—The Indian experience, World Bank Staff working paper No. 620, Washington, 1983.
7. Devi Rajula "Industrialisation Holds Key to Rural Development Kurukshetra, December, 1984, p. 34.
8. Indian Institute of Management, Evaluation of DIC programme Andhra Pradesh, Bangalore, May, 1988.
9. Government of India. Report of the Committee on unemployment (Bhagavati Committee, New Delhi) (1973).
10. Bepin Behari. Rural Industrialisation in India, Vikas Publishing House, New Delhi (1976).
11. Banujam, K.V. (1964), Poverty Alleviation through Rural Industrialisation, Kurukshetra (India's Journal of Rural Development) Vol. XXXIII No, 1 October, (1984) p.p. 51-53.
12. Rathnam, N.V. (1984). Rural Industrialisation and IRDP Kurukshetra (India's Journal of Rural Development) Vol. XXXIII No.3, December, (1984) pp. 4-8.

13. Myrdal Gunnar : Asian Drama, An Enquiry into the poverty of nations, the penguin press, London. (1968).
14. Sen, A.K., Employment, Technology and Development, Oxford. (1975).
15. Johnson Harry, G.,. Technology and Economic interdependence. (1975)
16. Vyasulu Vinod (1976). Technology and change in underdeveloped societies Economic and political weekly, August, 28 (1975).
17. Raj Krishna. Rural Unemployment policies for the fifth plan, Economic and Political Weekly, March, 3. (1973).
18. Tin Bergen, J. Discussion in Manar Hada (Ed) problems of unemployment in India, Allied Publishers, p.7.
19. Mathur, Gautam, True employment and Non employment in D.L. Naryana et. al., (Eds), Planning for employment, Sterling Publishers. (1980) pp. 1-9.
20. Wu, Jageh. Capital Intensity and Economic Growth under developed countries, Ising Hua Journal of Chinese studies, New series, III-IV (1968) pp 219-245.
21. Minocha, A.C. Industrial Development in M.P. Regional structure and strategy for employment oriental industrialisation in D.L. Narayana et al., (Eds) O.Peit (1980) pp. 259-3007.
22. Rastogi, K.M., Employment Generation through S.S.V. and C.I. A case study of M.P. in D.L. Naryana et al., (Eds), op cit, pp. 308-320.
23. UNIDO SSI in Lain America, Publication No. 111337, (1969) p. 56.
24. Government of India, Planning Commission (1956). Report of the Committee on village and SSI (Chairman), D.G. Karve).
25. Rostagi, K.M., Employment Generation through S.S. Village and Cottage Industries, A case study of M.P. in D.L. Narayana et al., (Eds). (1980).
26. Government of India, Report of the Committee on unemployment (Bhagavati Committee), New Delhi. (1973).

2

Small-Scale Industries in India

Policies, Programmes and Performance

Introduction

Over the years, the Government of Developing countries have adopted positive measures to defeat the forces of stagnation. To perform this gigantic task, a well-considered and most suited policy of economic development has been framed. The growth process of these countries aims at accelerating the economic development to enhance the social welfare. Infact, the economic change is a part of a wider social change and the economic development is a long-term process of intrinsic growth. Therefore, the task of policy making has a vital role to play in selecting the desired objectives and suitable alternatives for stimulating the economic growth. It also requires a careful examination of the existing institutional framework, social values, economic requirements and their implications, keeping in view, the need for rapid social and economic development of the economy.

Now-a-days, most of the developing countries are following the thesis that industrialisation is a process of growth and as such is organically linked both to the social and economic past and to the parallel processes of social and economic development.[1] The thesis reaffirms the importance of industrialisation as an effective means for solving the problems of economic and social progress in developing countries of the world.

Since the end of the Second World War, most of the developing countries are giving top priority to industrialisation. Actually, the planners of most of the developing countries have regarded industrialisation as the panacea for underdevelopment and poverty. The most primitive economies are now keenly interested in rapidly enlargely manufacturing industry. It is in rapid industrialisation "in which they place a major hope of finding a solution to their problems of poverty, insecurity and over-population and ending their newly realised backwardness in the modern world.[2]

The poor countries believe that industrialisation brings some basic changes in the production-functions and techniques, occupational structure and the level of activities in the other sectors of the economy. These changes will remove the obstacles which were retarding the growth and will raise the standard of living. Gunnar Myrdal has rightly pointed out the relationship of industrialization to economic development when he observes "the manufacturing industry represents, in a sense, a higher stage of production in advanced countries. The development of manufacturing has been concomitant with these countries, spectacular economic progress and rise in the levels of living. Not least in the underdeveloped countries, the productivity in industry tends to be considerably greater than in the traditional agricultural pursuits.

In the light of the aforesaid facts, it cannot be denied that industrialisation, in general, can be the best means of achieving the higher growth rate and raising the living standards of the people. In the context of the developing economies, a few a specific objects and policies of industrialisation have been generally agreed to by the planners. They are to provide work for growing populations, to raise the standard of living by increasing the per capita, net national income and often to improve balance of the payments situations."[3] Thus the development of small-scale industries alone can provide large-scale employment to the growing population in developing countries.

Role of Small-Scale Industries in Industrialisation of India

India is often described as an underdeveloped country. The term underdeveloped implies that the resources human and material of the country have not been properly harnessed with the result that the people have to live in poverty. They are under fed and physically weak and their working capacity is low. Underdevelopment implies that the level of real income and capital per head of population is low as judged by the standards in developed countries of North America and Western Europe. In under developed countries, there is no large-scale application of the fruits of scientific and technological advances to agriculture and industry. Subsistence production is generally important for the people, the markets are comparatively narrow and manufacturing is usually unimportant.[4]

In many developing countries, manpower is relatively abundant. It is, therefore, imperative that their full and effective utilisation should become a focal point of socio-economic policies. Emphasis has to be laid on small-scale industries to absorb the surplus manpower in these countries.

The concept, small-scale industry covers a wide range of activities and its definition changed from time to time. The latest definition (July, 1990) of small-scale industries is quite broad based. All industries with a capital investment of Rs. 20 lakhs in plant and machinery are classified as small-scale industries. The smaller units with a capital investment of Rs. 2 lakhs in plant and machinery are classified as tiny units. Units with a capital investment in plant and machinery varying between Rs. 20 lakhs and Rs. 25 lakhs are classified as ancillary industries.

The development of small-scale sector has been important in India because of the following reasons: First, the small-scale unit requires less capital outlay and at the same time, it provides more employment than the large-scale sector. Sector, a small-scale unit does not require highly sophisticated technology. It can, therefore, be useful in backward areas where the people have yet to be trained to meet the challenge of sophisticated technology.

Importance of Small-Scale Industries

Apart from their inherent usefulness in terms of numerical superiority, small-scale industries play a vital role in the economic growth of developing countries as discussed below:

(i) Utilisation of Resources

Small-Scale Industries facilitate the tapping of resources

which otherwise would remain unused. These resources include entrepreneurship, capital labour and raw materials. They can mobilize rural savings which may otherwise remain idle or may be spent on luxuries or channelled into non-productive ventures.

(ii) Employment Generation

Since they are fairly labour-intensive small-scale industries create employment opportunities at a relatively low-capital cost. In India, there is basic problem of absorbing the surplus manpower in non-agricultural jobs and providing additional employment opportunities for the growing population.

(iii) Generation of Foreign Exchange

Small-Scale Industries facilitate, substantial foreign exchange savings and earnings. A wide range of consumer and simple produced goods, now being imported, can be economically produced domestically on a small-scale basis as long as adequate facilities are provided.

(iv) Diversification of Industrial Structures

Small-Scale Industries contribute significantly to the strengthening of the industrial structure. Many more articles can be produced economically by the small-scale than that of large scale industries.

(v) Entrepreneurial Development

Small-Scale Industries serve as seedbeds of entrepreneurship. They serve the developing economy not only by their output of goods but also by functioning as a nursery of entrepreneurial and managerial talent. This role of small-scale Industries is of decisive importance in any economy where the industrial structure consists of the few large-scale and medium sized ones, on the one hand, and of large numbers of traditional industries such as artisan units, handicrafts and cottage industries on the other.

(vi) Regional Development and Industrial Dispersal

The concentration of industrial and other activities has given birth to the phenomenon of the so called pockets of development where economic and social change is achieved at much faster rate than in the outlaying rural districts.

This trend, although predominant, can be checked and corrected through the establishment of small-scale industries. For one thing, such industries lead to the creation of employment opportunities on a dispersed basis not only in large cities and towns but also in smaller towns and far flung regions. The establishment of small-scale industries would, therefore, make it possible to reverse the current trend of the migration of the people form rural to urban areas.

Small-Scale Industry and Industrial Policy Resolution

A study of the industrial policy documents reveals that small-scale industrial unit has been assigned an important role throughout the period since Indian political independence. Thus, for example protection and promotion of small-scale industry has all along been listed as a major objective in all of the industrial policy documents. The policy statements also indicate the lines on which the Government has been taking or contemplating concrete steps.

The point may be highlighted by referring to the Industrial Policy resolution:

Industrial Policy Resolution, 1948

This policy Resolution (1948) recognized the fact that cottage and small-scale industries have a very important role in the national economy, offering as they do give scope for individual, village or co-operative enterprise and means for the rehabilitation of displaced persons. These industries are particularly suited for better utilisation of local resources and for the achievement of local self sufficiency in respect of certain types of essential consumer goods like food, cloth and agricultural implements. The healthy expansion of cottage and small-scale industries depend upon a number of factors like the provision of raw materials, cheap power, technical advice, organised marketing of their produce, and where necessary, safeguards against the intensive competition by large-scale manufacture, as well as on the education of the workers in the use of best available technique.

Industrial Resolution, 1956

This Resolution Policy of the Government of India 1956 stressed the role of cottage, village and small-scale industries in the development of the National economy. In relation to some of the problems that need urgent solutions, offer some distinct advantages. They provide immediate large-scale employment. They offer a method of ensuring a more equitable distribution of the national income and facilitate an effective mobilisation of resources of capital and skill which might otherwise remain unutilised. Some of the problems that unplanned urbanization tend to create will be avoided by the establishment of small centres of industrial production all over the country.

The Government of India has been following a policy of supporting cottage and small-scale industries by restricting the volume of production in the large-scale sector, by differential taxation or by direct subsides. While such measures will continue to be taken, whenever necessary, the aim of the State policy will be to ensure that the decentralised sector acquired sufficient to be self supporting its development integrated with that of large-scale industry.

Industrial Policy Resolution, 1977

The importance assigned to small-scale industry is emphasised in still greater measure in the 1977. Industrial Policy Resolution.

The emphasis of Industrial Policy before the adoption of Industrial Policy Resolution was mainly on large industries neglecting cottage industries completely giving minor role to small-scale industries. The firm policy of the Government was to change this approach. The main aim of the new industrial policy was the effective promotion of cottage and small-scale industries widely dispersed in rural areas and small towns.

From the greater emphasis laid on the small-scale industry by 1977 Resolution, big push has been given to the growth of the decentralised sector. Thus, for example the list of industries reserved for this sector has been expanded to cover 304 items for the earlier list of 180 items (since then the list has been further expanded to cover in all over 807 items). The statement also declared the intention of the Government to provide maximum support to the small-scale industries for product standardisation quality control, marketing etc., on priority basis. Within the small-scale sector a sub sector of tiny units has been created and this sub sector was expected to receive preferential treatment even within small-scale sector.

It was also proposed in the statement to enact special legislation for protecting the interest of cottage and household industries. Each district to have one agency called the "District Industries Centre" to deal with the requirements of this industry. A separate wing to be created in the Industrial Development Bank of India for Small-Scale Industries to provide effective financial support to this sector. Finally, special efforts use envisaged for modernising Khadi and village industries and for promoting appropriate technologies all round.

Industries Policy Resolution, 1980

The Industrial Policy statement made by Government of India on 23rd July, 1980 primarily sought to harmonise the growth in the small-scale sector with that in the large and medium sector. The emphasis in the new policy was on fostering the complementarity between the large and small sectors so that the new dichotomizes (which are more apparent than real) between the two sectors did not distort the economic pattern.

The board socio-economic objectives of the New Industrial Policy of 1980 were set out as follows:[5]

i) Optimum utilisation of installed capacity.

ii) Maximising production and achieving higher productivity.

iii) Higher employment generation:

iv) Correction of regional imbalances through a preferential development of industrially backward areas.

v) Strengthening of the agricultural base by according a preferential treatment to agro-based industries and promoting optimum inter sectoral relationship;

vi) Faster promotion of export oriented and import substitution industries;

vii) Promoting economic federalism with an equitable spread of investment and the dispersal of returns amongst widely spread small but growth units in rural as well as urban areas.

viii) Consumer protection against high prices and bad quality.

An important element of the new policy was the raising of the investment limits of the tiny and small-scale sectors. These limits were redefined in terms of investment in plant and machinery and were fixed at Rs. 2 lakhs for tiny sector instead of Rs. 1 lakh Rs. 20 lakhs for the small-scale sector instead of rs. 10 lakhs and Rs. 25 lakhs instead of Rs. 15 lakhs for ancillaries. This step was essentially a pragmatic one and took into account the significant price rise that occurred in the last five years following the fixation of the investment limits for the small-scale sector.

This decision would, it was hoped, bring into the fold of the small-scale sector, a number of technology oriented units whose growth would be backed by a suitable system of incentives. The new industrial policy spelt out some of these incentives which was proposed to be provided so that the small-scale sector might grow in a significant measure and contribute to the national economy.

The policy statement of 1980 made it clear that the existing support programme for marketing as well as the reservation of items in the small-scale sector would continue. The basis thrust of this policy was to ensure a continued growth of the small-scale sector without at the same time, inhibiting the growth of other sectors. In this context, automatic growth for a large number of industries in the medium and large sector would be ensured so that they could grow without hindrance.

A special emphasis was laid on the establishment of nucleus plants in backward districts around which a programme of ancialiarisation would be developed. To quote from the statement: "The proposed nucleus plants in industrially backward district would generate a net work of small scale units, or the existing net work of small scale units in the an area would acquire a faster growth by the coming up of a nucleus plant in the area. In between the nucleus large plants and the satellite ancillaries, the Government would permit a system of linkages for an integrated industrial development.[6] The new policy targets set for the sixth plan viz., production of the value of more than Rs. 35,000 crores, employment of 11 million persons and with promotion of exports totalling nearly Rs. 2,000 crores. The small-scale sector might look forward to a steady and balanced growth within the frame work of the new policy statement of the Government of India.

Industrial Policy (1990)

The Government has been considering the need to take measures for promotion of small-scale and agro based industries and to change procedures for grant of industrial approvals.

Main Objectives

2. In pursuance of Industrial policy to re-orient industrial growth to serve the objective of employment generation, dispersal of industry in rural areas and to enhance the contribution of small-scale industries to exports, it has been decided to take the measure enumerated below.

Investment Ceiling for Small-Scale and Ancillary Units

3. The investment ceiling in plant and machinery for small-scale industries (fixed in 1985) would be raised from the present Rs. 35 lakhs to Rs. 60 lakhs and correspondingly, for ancillary units, from Rs. 45 lakhs to Rs. 75 lakhs. In order to enable small-scale industries to play an important role in the total export effort, the small-scale units which undertake to export at least 30% of the annual production by the third year will be permitted to step up their investment in plant and machinery to Rs. 75 lakhs.

Tiny Units

4. Investment ceiling in respect of tiny units would also be increased from the present Rs. 2 lakhs to Rs. 5 lakhs. However, with regard to their locations, the population limit of 50,000 as per 1981 census would continue to apply. Steps will be taken to ensure better in flow of credit and other vital inputs and to improve infrastructural support to the constituents to the tiny sector.

Reservation Items

5. Presently, 836 items have been reserve for exclusive manufacture in the small-scale sector. Efforts be made to identify more items enable to similar reservation. Encroachment and violation by large-scale units into areas, reserved for small-scale sector will be effectively dealt with.

Central Investment Subsidy

6. A new scheme of Central Investment subsidy exclusively for the small-scale sector in rural and backward areas capable of generating higher level of employment at lower capital cost would be implemented.

Upgradation of Technology

7. With a view to improving the competitiveness of the

products manufactured in the small-scale sector, programmes for modernisation and upgradation of technology would be implemented. A number of technology centres, tool rooms, process and product development centres, testing centres, etc. will be set up under the umbrella of an apex technology development centre in the Small Industries Development Organisation (SIDO).

Flow of Credit

8. To ensure adequate and timely flow of credit for small-scale industries, a new apex bank known as Small Industries Development Bank of India (SIDBI) has already been established. One of the major tasks of SIDBI and other commercial banks/financial institutions would be to channelise need-based, higher flow of credit, both by way of term loan and working capital, to the tiny and rural industrial. A targeted approach will be adopted to ensure implementation and to facilitate monitoring this objective.

Review of Fiscal Concessions

9. The existing regime of fiscal concessions will be reviewed, both to provide sustained support to the units in the small-scale sector and to remove the incentives for their graduation and further growth.

Identification of Locations

10. An exercise will be undertaken to identify locations in rural areas endowed with adequate power supply and intensive campaigns will be launched to attract suitable entrepreneurs, to prove all other inputs and foster small-scale and tiny industries. Similarly, industries which are not energy intensive will be identified for proliferation in rural areas where power supply is presently a constraint.

11. In order to widen the entrepreneurial base, the Government would lay particular emphasis on training a women and youths under the entrepreneurial development programme. A special cell would be established in Small Industries Development Organisation (SIDO) and state directorates of industries to assist women entrepreneurs.

Relaxation in Bureaucratic Controls

12. One of the persistent complaints of the small-scale units

is their being subjected to a large number of acts/laws, being required to maintain a number of registers, submits plethora of returns and face an army of inspector, particularly in the field of labour legislations. These bureaucratic controls will be reduced so that unnecessary interference is eliminated. Further procedures will be simplified and paper work cut down.

Expansion in Activities of KVIC and KVI Board

13. In order to assist the large number of artisans engaged in rural and cottage industries, activities of the Khadi and Village Industries Commissions (KVIC) and KVI board will be expanded and these organisations will be strengthened to discharge the responsibility more effectively. Special marketing organisations at the Central and State levels shall be created to assist rural artisans in marketing their products and also in supply of raw materials. Besides providing concessional credit, training facilities and free consultancy to groups of artisans will also be provided.

Agro Processing Industries

14. In agro processing industries, greater success has been achieved where growers and processors have been integrated, as in the case of sugar. For the success of other agro-based industries also, close links must be forged between the growers and processor units. Industrial policy will, therefore, especially promote projects which are organised in close co-operation the basis of joint ownership. Growers will be encouraged to set up processing units within the framework of co-operative societies or similar institutional frame work. This will also ensure the transmission of better technology for enhanced agriculture production.

15. In sectors where units require licensing, the policy will also encourage location of processing units in rural areas here growers are concentrated. Apart from economic benefits of the proximity to raw materials it will help in dispersal of industry and increasing employment in rural areas.

16. Agro-processing industry will receive high priority in credit allocation from the financial institutions. In apportionment of working capital banks will give higher priority to such industries as compared to the rest of the industrial sector.

17. In order to bring the best technology available to these industries, technology approvals will be given within 30 days of presentation to the Secretariat for Industrial Approvals in the Department of Industrial Development. Government will actively promote and generate adoption of new technologies in the field.

Procedures for Industrial Approvals

18. Indian industry must be made more competitive internationally. It also needs to be released from unnecessary bureaucratic shackles by reducing the number of clearances required from the Government. While the Government will continue to examine large projects in view of resource constraints, decisions in respect of medium sized investments will be left to the entrepreneurs. To achieve these objectives, the following decisions have been taken.

Delicensing

19. All new units up to an investment of Rs. 25 crores in fixed assets in non-backward areas and Rs. 75 crores in centrally notified backward areas will be exempt from requirement of obtaining licence/registration.

Capital Goods (C.G.)

20. For the import of capital goods, the entrepreneur would have entitlement to import up to a landed value of 30 per cent of the total value of plant and machinery required for the unit.

Raw Materials and Components

21. For import of raw materials and components, imports will be permissible up to a landed value of 30 per cent of the ex-factory value of annual production. The ex-factory value of. production. The ex-factory value of production will exclude the excise duty on the item of production. Raw materials and components on OGL will not be included with this 30 per cent limit. For all licensable items of raw material and components, import licensing procedures will continue to operate,

Foreign Collaboration

22. In respect of transfer of technology, if import of technology is considered necessary by the entrepreneur, he can enter in to an agreement with the collaborator, without

obtaining any clearance from the Government, provided that royalty payment does not exceed 5 per cent on domestic sales and 8 per cent of exports. If, however, lumpsum payment is involved in the import of technology, the proposal will require Government clearance, but a decision will be communicated to the entrepreneur within a period of 30 days.

Foreign Investment

23. Keeping in view the need to attract effective inflow of technology, investment up to 40 per cent of equity will be allowed on an automatic basis. In such proposals also, the landed value of important C.G. shall not exceed 30 per cent of value of plant and machinery.

Minimum Economic Size

24. In order to ensure that investment leads to production of goods that attain international competitiveness and that maximum efficiency is ensured, the unit would have to confirm to the minimum economic size in cases where such a size has been prescribed.

Expansion

25. The de-regulation suggested above would cover all cases of expansion and would not be restricted only to new units.

Board Banding

26. The existing Board Banding Scheme would continue to be in force. In addition, if no extra investment is required, no clearance from the Government would be necessary for production and sale of any new item by existing units. This would not include those items which are reserved for small-scale industries.

Location Policy and Environmental Clearance

27. The location policy would not be applied to such industries by the Centre except for location in and around metropolitan cities location will not be permissible within 20 Km. calculated from the periphery of the metropolitan area except in prior designated industrial areas and for non-polluting industries such as electronics, computer software and printing. It will be up to State Governments to regulate indus-

trial locations keeping in mind local conditions and requirements and their respective spatial development plans and zoning and town planning laws. Similarly, environmental clearance would have to be obtained from the prescribed authority at the state level. In future, Central legislation should introduce new provisions, that law would automatically to these units as well.

Export Oriented Units

28. 100 per cent export oriented units (EOUs) and units to be set up in export processing zones (EPZs) are also being delicensed under the scheme up to an investment limit of rs. 75 crores.

Convertibility Clause

29. Such investments shall be exempted from the "convertibility clause" applicable to financing by Indian Financial Institutions.

30. It may be clarified that in the application of the proposals for exemption. 836 items which are reserved for production in the small-scale sector will continue to be excluded.

31. The above proposals will be applicable to all manufacturing items in a specified list. The list shall follow the nomenclature of the Indian trade classification based on the harmonised system. In each section of the classification, apart from positive mention of approved items, those not permissible shall be specifically excluded from the benefit of the proposals listed above. Approval for excluded items will be as per the existing industrial policy regime and procedures.

32. Units set up by MRTP/FERA companies will be covered by the procedures set out above, but they will continue to reed clearances under the provisions and regulations of these two acts.

33. The existing De-licensed Industries Scheme, Exempted Industries Scheme and BCTD Registration System will stand abolished.

Development of Small-Scale Industries during Plan period

Till independence, only cottage industries, village industries, rural industries or agro-based industries were considered to be small industries. The National Planning Committee, set up in 1938 under the chairmanship of Pandit Jawaharlal Nehru, constituted a panel to study this problem. With the dawn of the planned era in the country, the Government has been following a policy of promotion as well as protection of the small industries sector but the protection would be gradually reduced as and when promotional activities began to produce results.

First Five Year Plan (1951-56)

In the First Five Year Plan, a major step taken for the development of village and small-scale industries was the establishment of All India Boards to advise and assist in the formulation of the programme of development of small-scale industries, including sericulture and coir. Although during the Second World War, Small Industries were set up throughout the country to meet the Defence requirements, a number of these disappeared totally or partially at the end of the war. The First Plan attempted to indicate some of the problems which were involved to formulation substantial development programmes for small industries and handicrafts and divided small industries into three groups viz., those which exist independently, those integrated with and those offering competition to, large scale industries, stores, purchase and replacement of imports were mentioned as the two directions in which the demand for products of small-scale production, establishment of new township as in the river valley projects and training, research and finance these were the aspects stressed.[7]

Second Five Year Plan (1956-61)

The total outlay on small-scale industries in the Second Five Year Plan was Rs. 180 crores as against Rs. 43 crores in the First Plan. A number of new programmes were organised and steps were taken to provide a more assured market for the products of some of the industries. Reservation of the production of certain varieties of cloth and certain type of agricultural implements, prohibition of further expansion in certain large-scale industries like vegetable oils, rice milling, leather foot were, match etc. and the laying down of separate targets of production for the small-scale and the large-scale sectors of certain industries like bicycles and sewing machines were some of the steps taken.

In the later period of the Second Plan, marketing conditions for the some of the small-scale industries improved following the intensification of import restrictions. Programmes for village and small-scale industries and problems connected with their implementation were reviewed by the Karva Committee on Village and Small-Scale Industries (Second Five Year Plan) which was appointed by the Planning Commission in June, 1955. The programme Evaluation Organisation made a study of rural industries in selected community development blocks. In spite of shortage of certain basic raw materials many small industries totally machine tools, sewing machines, electric fans and motors, bicycles, builders hardware and hand tools expanded considerably at the rate of 25 per cent to 50 per cent per annum. The number of registered companies with authorities capital of less than Rs. 5 lakhs each and engaged in processing and manufacturing increased by 1,160 during 1957-1961. Sixty industrial estate were completed, and the programme for small-scale industries as a whole provided full time employment to 3 lakh persons.[8]

Third Five Year Plan (1961-1966)

The main objectives of the Third Five Year Plan in regard to the programme for village and small-scale industries were:[9]

i) To improve the productivity of the workers and reduce production costs by placing a relatively greater emphasis on positive forms of assistance, such as improvement in skill, supply of technical advice, better equipment and credit.

ii) To reduce progressively the role of subsidies, sales, rebates and sheltered markets.

iii) To promote the growth of industries in rural areas and in small towns.

iv) To promote the development of small-scale industries as ancillaries to large industries, and

v) To organise artisans and craftsmen on co-operative lines.

In the Third Five Year Plan (1961-66) a total outlay of Rs. 264 crores was proposed for programmes of village and small industries, made up to Rs. 141 crores for scheme of the States and Union territories and Rs. 123 crores for the centre and centrally sponsored programmes and schemes. In addition, Rs. 273 crores were expected to be invested from private sources, including banking institutions and Rs. 20 crores on the programmes of community development, rehabilitation of displaced persons, social welfare and welfare of backward classes. Part time and fuller employment was envisaged for 8 million persons, and additional full time employment for 6.3 lakh persons during the Third Plan.

Fourth Five Year Plan (1969-1974)

The Fourth Five Year Plan (1969-74) proposed a total outlay of Rs. 370 crores in the public sector for the development of village and small industries, exclusive of the outlays on the development of these industries in the programmes for community development, rehabilitation of displaced persons and development of special areas. About Rs. 400 crores were expected to be invested from private sources, including banking institutions. Thus, a total outlay of nearly Rs. 800 crores was expected to be available for small-scale industries under the Fourth Plan.

The main programme during the Fourth Plan were to entrust the work of administration of credit facilities under the State Aid to Industries Act, training and common service facilities, quality marketing and consolidation of the Industrial Estates Programme, to the States. The Central Government continued to implemented schemes related to industrial research, industrial extension services, supply of machines on hire purchase terms etc.[10]

Fifth Five Year Plan (1974-179)

A significantly large number of persons, dependent on traditional industries like handloom, sericulture, coir, khadi and village industries, living below the poverty line, live mostly concentrated in rural and backward areas, some of them belong to the backward classes. Therefore, the principal objectives of the programme for the development of different small industries in the Fifth Plan were to facilitate the attainment of some of the major tasks for the removal of poverty and inequality in the consumption standards of these persons through the creation of large-scale opportunities for fuller and additional productive employment and improvement in their skills so as to raise their level of earnings. Further more, the programme was reoriented to set up the production of some of the beside and essential articles for the masses and of the products which have a larger potential for exports. Taking into account the shortcomings in the implementation of the programmes during the Fourth Plan Period and the recommendations of the

Task Forces set up in connection with the formulation of the programmes for these industries, the broad strategy of the programmes was.[11]

1. To develop and promote entrepreneurship and provide a package of consultancy service so as to generate the maximum opportunities for employment, particularly self-employment.
2. To facilitate a fuller utilisation of skills and equipment of the persons already engaged in different small industries.
3. To progressively improve the production techniques of these industries so as to bring them to a viable level, and
4. To promote these industries in selected growth centres in semi urban and rural areas, including backward area.

Sixth Five Year Plan (1980-85)

The Sixth Five Year Plan marked a significant stage in the development of small-scale industry.

The promotion of village and small-scale industries was to continue to be an important element in the national development strategy because of its very favorable capital output ratio and high employment intensity. During the sixth five year plan, the programmes for the village and small industries sector were framed with the following objectives.[12]

i) improvement in the levels of production and earnings, particularly in the earnings of artisans, by upgrading skills and technologies and producer oriented marketing.

ii) creating of additional employment opportunities on a dispersed and decentralised basis.

iii) ensuring a significant contribution to growth in the manufacturing sector through, inter alia, a fuller utilisation of existing installed capacities.

iv) the establishment of a wider entrepreneurial base by providing appropriate training and a package of incentives.

v) creation of a viable structure of the village and small industries sector so as to progressively reduce the role of subsidies; and

vi) Expand efforts in export promotion.

In the light of above objectives, the policy support for the development programmes relating to village and small industries during the Sixth Five Year Plan was along to the following lines:

i) integration of the promotional programme in the sector with other area development programmes, and the adoption of a cluster approach, particularly for the traditional industries.

ii) restructuring of the organisational base at the district level to make it more effective and result oriented.

iii) development of appropriate technologies and skills, their effective extension and transmission.

iv) increased availability of raw materials, including the creation of buffer stocks, particulars of critical raw materials.

v) accelerated flow of institutional funds, specially in favour of artisans, village industries and tiny units, and the rationalization of the interest rate structure:

vi) organization of producer - oriented marketing both within and outside the country.

vii) selective reservation of items for exclusive production in and purchase from the cottage and small industries.

viii) effective promotion of ancillaries;

ix) strengthening and extension of the co-operative form of organisation, particularly for the cottage and tiny units and

x) building up of a sound data base to facilitate proper policy formulation and evaluation.

As a major contributor to the planned growth of employment, the small-scale sector was to receive a very high priority. The development effort would be mounted on many fronts. If necessary, certain products would be reserved for manufacture exclusively in the small-scale sector and excise duty differentials will ensure that the products of the small-scale sector are cheaper for the public than similar products manufactured by the small-scale sector.

To ensure a co-ordinated growth and minimise for number of contact points, District Industries Centres were to be set up. The transfer of research and technology to this sector was given much greater impetus. As for credit, the possibility of extending the margin money scheme was considered. In the marketing of products, a major effort was mounted to remove the middleman and to provide, through the co-operative sector, a remunerative outlet for the products of cottage industries. Steps would be taken to enhance the provision for training, technical assistance and other facilities.

The outlay on village and small-scale industries was stepped up from Rs. 535.03 crores in the Fifth Plan to Rs. 1,780-45 crores in the Sixth Plan. Production targets for this sector have also been stepped up from Rs. 33,150 crores to Rs. 49,235 crores. Moreover, this sector was expected to create additional employment of 90 lakhs, raising the total to 326 lakhs. Exports use expected to increase from Rs. 2,225 crores in 1979-80 to Rs. 3,685 crores. It was estimated that the total exports during the Sixth Plan would be of the order of about Rs. 15,500 crores.

The outlays for the development of small-scale industries in the successive Five Year Plans are shown in the Table 2.1.

Seventh Five Year Plan (1985-90)

Within the overall focus on food, work and productivity laid down in the Seventh Five Year Plan the village and small industries sector would contribute towards improving the economic and occupational profile of the rural - semi urban and weaker sections of urban communities through promotion of village and small-scale industrial activities.[14]

The implementation of the Seventh Plan started in 1985-86. On completion of half the term of Plan, a mid-term appraisal was made and placed before the parliament on 22/23 March, 1988.

For promotion of rural industrialisation Khadi village industries centres reorganised and professionalised. Further specific steps were taken to diversify industries in rural areas to remove regional in balances have resulted in about 43.5 per cent of all industrial licences granted to backward area during the first two years.[15]

Research and development efforts were stepped up and the results thereof were transferred to the field level agencies, providing for some of the welfare measures including housing-cum-workshed facilities and thrift fund scheme for the benefit of the artisan type of units had been considered. In this plan period, the government started extending the basic support in terms of functional assistance like marketing, ancillarisation, credit flow, supply of raw material and critical inputs, technology, training etc. The Seventh Plan envisaged discouraging the setting up of industries on or around urban agglomerations and package of incentives were provided to attract industries in backward regions. The implementing agencies did set up cells in monitor, evaluate and build an effective information service systems so as to enable a periodic assessment of various promotional programmes.

Public Sector Outlays and Plan Provisions for Village and Small Industries

The public sector investment for fostering the village and small industries (VSI) during the plan era is shown in Table 2.1 absolute terms the investment, in village and small industries sector has increased from plan to plan.

Table 2.1 : Plan-wise Allocation for Village and Small Industries

Sl. No.	*Plan*	*VSI*	*Outlay for Industry*	*Total Plan*	*USI as %age of industry outlay*	*USI as %age of total plan outlay*
1.	First	42	97	1,960	43.30	2.1
2.	Second	187	1,125	4,672	16.62	4.0
3.	Third	341	1,967	8,577	12.25	2.8
4.	Fourth	243	3,107	15,779	7.82	1.5
5.	Fifth	592	9,581	39,426	6.18	1.5
6.	Sixth	1,980	17,290	1,09,646	11.45	1.8
7.	Seventh	2,753	22,461	1,80,000	12.26	1.5

Source : 1. For First Plan to Sixth Plan 25 Years of KVIC Commerce Vol. 144, No. 3692, pp. 3950.

2. For Seventh Plan, Government of India, Seventh Five Year Plan 1985–90, Planning Commission, New Delhi, Vol. II, 1985 p. 10.4.

But its proportionate share in industrial and total plan out lays has gone down from nearly 43 per cent and 2.1 per cent in the First Plan to 12.26 per cent 1.5 per cent in the Seventh Plan respectively. The outlays in village and small industries sector have dwindled during the plan period.

Table 2.2 : Plan-wise Production, Employment, Sales and Earnings in Village Industries

Sl. No.	*Plan*	*Production* (Rs. in crores	*Employment* (in lakh persons)	*Sales* (Rs. in crores)	*Earnings* (Rs. in crores)
1.	First	10.93 (100.00)	3.02 (100.00)	0.90 (100.00)	3.60 (100.00)
2.	Second	33.16 (303.00)	5.64 (187.00)	28.36 (3151.00)	6.53 (181.00)
3.	Third	55.87 (%11.00)	8.75 (290.00)	49.73 (5526.00)	10.74 (298.00)
4.	Fourth	122.00 (1116.00)	9.27 (307.00)	115.64 (12840.00)	22.15 (616.00)
5.	Fifth	347.98 (3184.00)	16.13 (534.00)	388.97 (43219.00)	78.84 (2190.00)
6.	Sixth	807.06 (7384.00)	24.84 (823.00)	880.46 (97829.00)	220.49 (6125.00)
7.	Seventh	1700.00 (1554.00)	30.00 (993.00)	1785.00 (1983.00)	320.00 (8889.00)

Note : Figures in parentheses indicate percentages with first plan figures as base.

Source : 1. For First Plan to Sixth Plan Report of KVIC/985–86 Bombay, 1986.

Seventh Plan, Government of India, Seventh Five Year Plan 1985-90, New Delhi, 1985. It is noticed from the table the production has increased from Rs. 10.93 crores to Rs. 807.06 crores. Employment from 3.02 lakh persons to 24.84 lakh persons, sales from Rs. 0.90 crores to RS. 880-86 crores and earnings from Rs. 3.6 crores to Rs. 320 crores during Fist Plan to Seventh Plan Period.

Eighth Five Year Plan

In the Eighth Five Year Plan, the Government's decision is to allocate 50 per cent of the plan investment to the Rural and Agricultural Development, shrinking of the plan size will mean even less of investment for the infrastructure especially power which is key input both for the agricultural and industrial development (i.e.) cottage and small-scale industries.

A major change proposed in the Eighth Plan is to redefine the Rural and Agricultural sector. There is a growing realisation that if these heads of expenditure are taken out of the purview of Rural and Agricultural development, which includes cottage and small-scale industries those are highly labour intensive through self employment are total allocation to these sectors will amount to more than 60 per cent of the total public sector investment.

Industrial Development in Backward Regions in India Policies and Programmes for the Development of Small-Scale Industries in India

The Small Industries have enough scope to exploit available local resources such as savings, raw materials, skilled and unskilled labour. Further. They generate income for consumption of wage goods and provide employment to the unemployed persons. So, it is necessary to allot public sector investment for development of infrastructural facilities and provide incentives through development programmes for setting up of small industries.

The Industrial Policy Resolution, 1948 stressed the need for development of Small-Scale Industries. The objectives of the policy are:

1. To establish a social order where justice and equality of opportunities could be assured.
2. To raise the standard of living of the people through exploitation of talents and available resources of the country.
3. To accelerate production to meet the needs of the growing population and
4. To provide more and more opportunities for employment. This policy was in force upto 1956.

During the First Five Year Plan, a major step was taken for the development of village and small industries. It was the establishment of six All India Boards to advise and assist the Government in the formulation of programmes for development of handloom industry, Khadi and Village industries, small-scale industries, Handicrafts, Sericulture. An International Team of experts was invited by the Government of India in 1953 to study the problems of the small-scale industries. The team recommended the establishment of Regional Small Industries Service Institutes. Accordingly favour such Institutes were set up at Bombay, Calcutta, Madurai and Faridabad with branch units in Uttar Pradesh, Bihar, Andhra Pradesh and Travancore Cochin. These Institutes provide various kinds of technical services to village and small industries, such as, information about improved techniques of production, technical advice and assistance in the utilization of the local raw materials[17]. The programme of work of Small-Scale Industries Board follows largely the lines indicated in the Report of the International Team. The main part of the programme was the establishment of a number of Institutes for organisation, technical servicing and business counselling and marketing assistance.

Industrial Estates

The Industrial Estate Programme was started in 1955 following the recommendation of the International Planning Team. Under this programme, suitable sites with all the facilities, such as water, electricity, transport, steam, communications, banks, post-office, raw materials depots, canteens, watch and wad, First Aid etc., are to be provided so as to create the necessary climate for the development of small industries. The main objectives of the Industrial Estate Programme are:

1. To shift the small-scale industries from congested areas to Industrial Estates with a view to increasing their productivity.
2. To achieve decentralised industrial development in small towns and villages and
3. To assist ancillary industries in the townships surrounding major industrial undertakings, both in the public and private sectors.[18]

The Government of India had given a big boost under different Five Years Plans by encouraging the establishment of Industrial Estates in the country. The expenditure incurred during the plan periods by the Central and State Government on Industrial Estates is presented below:

Table 2.3 : Expenditure incurred on Industrial estates in India

(Rs. in crores)

Sl. No.	*Plan*	*Period*	*S.S.I.*	*Industrial*	*Total*
1.	First	1951–56	5.20	0.58	5.78
2.	Second	1956–61	44.40	11.60	56.00
3.	Third	1961–66	90.91	22.15	113.06
4.	Annual	1966–69	45.90	7.58	53.48
5.	Fourth	1969–74	80.46	15.73	96.19
6.	Fifth	1974–79	196.12	25.62	221.74
7.	Annual	1979–80	95.69	9.12	104.81
8.	Sixth	1980–85	561.74	54.36	616.10
9.	Seventh	1985–90	—	—	1120.51

Source : Government of India, Development Commissioner, Small-Scale Industries, New Delhi, Ministry of Industry.

From the above Table 2.3 it can be observed that the expenditure incurred for the development of industrial estates has increased significantly from a mere Rs. 0.58 crores in Fist Plan to RS. 54.36 crores in the Sixth Plan. It indicates that the amount spent for industrial infrastructure has increased impressively.

Industrial Development of Backward Areas

A serious thought was given by our policy makers, after Independence to make all the regions industrially developed so that greater employment opportunities and economic advocations can be provided to the people. The Government, since 1968, has been specially trying to stimulate the industrialisation of the backward areas. As a sequence to this policy decision, the Central Government appointed two Committees popularly known as "Pande Committee"[19] and "Wanchoo Committee"[20] Pande Committee was asked to go into the aspect of identifying industrially backward states and backward districts in the States, while the Wanchoo Committee was asked to suggest the financial and physical incentives to be given for promotion of new industries in industrially backward states. The Planning Commission approved the recommendations made by these Committees, with certain modifications as per the decisions taken by the National Development

Council. Finally, the Planning Commission in consultation with the financial institutions recommended to the State Government for implementation of the schemes of concessional finance and fiscal incentives. As a result, 246 districts all over the country were now eligible for concessional finance under the scheme. Out of these, 102 districts or areas have been selected for Central Investment Subsidy. Under the scheme of Backward Area Development, certain facilities, such as capital investment, subsidy, transport subsidy, credit, machinery on hire-purchase and also state incentives were provided by the Government directly or through some agencies for promotion of small-scale industries in backward areas.

The Central Government Capital Investment Subsidy Scheme was introduced in 1971, after considering the recommendations of Wanchoo Committee by the National Development Council Under this scheme, new or expanding units in selected backward districts were entitled to 10% subsidy on the total fixed capital or additional fixed capital investment upto Rs. 50 lakhs. However units with investment exceeding this ceiling would also be considered at the discretion of the Government, though the maximum amount of subsidy would still be Rs. 5 lakh. In 1973, the rate of subsidy was raised to 15% the investment ceiling to rs. 1 crore. The discretionary clause for Units with investment exceeding this limit would still hold, subject to a subsidy limit of Rs. 15 lakhs.

Simultaneously with the capital investment subsidiary, a transport subsidy scheme was also introduced in 1971 to develop industries in hilly backward areas. Under this scheme, new industrial units in the states and Union Territories of Jammu and Kashmir, Assam, Manipur, Meghalaya, Nagaland, Tripura, Arunachal Pradesh, Mizoram, Andaman and Nicobar Islands, Lakshadeep, Himachal Pradesh and the hilly districts of uttar Pradesh were eligible to a subsidy amounting to 50% of the transportation costs of both raw materials and finished goods. Expanding units were also eligible for this subsidy for their expansion programmes, provided that the increase in production exceeded 25% of average annual output during the last three years.

Credit facilities do have a vital role in the implementation of small industries development programme. The availability of required credit on easy and liberal terms is also essential for the progress of small industries. To achieve this, sound institutional framework is essential for the flow of credit to the small industries. The existing institutional framework for the flow of financial assistance to the small-scale industries sector consists of Banks (Commercial Banks, Co-operative Banks and Regional Rural Banks), State financial Corporations (SFC's), National Small Industries Corporation (NSIC) and State Small-Scale Industries Development Corporation (SSIDC). The Industrial Development Bank of India (IDBI) provides funds to the Commercial Banks and State Financial Corporations (SFC's) through refinancing and bills rediscounting schemes.

The Industrial Development Bank of India set up a Small and Village Industries Wing in 1978 to evolve appropriate policy framework to identify action areas for promoting the growth of the small and village industries and to monitor the credit facilities offered by various agencies of this sector. The refinance facility of Industrial Development Bank of India (IDBI) was and is even now Channelled through 180 primary lending institutions, which comprise 70 scheduled Commercial Banks, 56 Regional Rural banks, 10 State Co-operative Banks, 18 State Finance Corporation, 24 SIDC's and two All India Financial Institutions.[22]

Industrialisation

Industrialization has been defined by Sutcliffe as a process which has invariably been the outcome or accompaniment of economic development," a set of policies, which more than any other set of policies is seen as a means towards economic development.[23] Industrialisation in a developing country has become inseparable part of development process. Planners and policy makers have viewed it as the most acceptable has been argued that in an underdeveloped country with a backward agriculture and vast population there is a little choice but to give priority to the development of industries. The establishment of new kind of society (Industrialised) is easier than reformation of old"[24]

It is so because, the Industrial Sector is more powerful in innovation which injects dynamism and brings about lasting increase in productivity of labour. "Industrialization not only influences the growth of national output and income but also influences the natural life and the social, political and cultural pattern". Industrialisation of a basically agricultural primary export oriented economy as seen as the means by which the chains of dependence forced during the colonical period could be broken matching the newly acquired political independence with economic independence.[25] For these newly freed underdeveloped countries, industrialisation was sought to bring great relief. "It was hoped that Industrialisation would bring social transformation, social equality, higher levels of employment, more equitable distribution of income and well balanced regional development".[26] Industrial development has further been acknowledged as a means to distribute employment, income and consumption between the various regions by giving special emphasis on industrialization of backward regions. In the opinion of Rosestein Rodan Industrialisation is the way of achieving a more equal distribution of income between different areas of the world by raising income in depressed areas at a higher rate than in rich areas.[27] What Rosenstien Rodan says in the context of world economy is also applicable to an individual country, suffering from the problems of inter regional as well as intra regional disparities in development. Development of Industries in backward regions, therefore has been accepted as a means to reduce regional disparities. It is because, in addition to its innovation and dynamism that it is more flexible than agriculture as far as location aspect is considered. Manufacturing activity which is not rooted to raw material can be located in any region even in area with poor natural endowment if it is economically feasible to serve objective. Moreover, manufacturing activities have better potentiality for generating employment directly and indirectly through their backward forward linkages with other sectors of the economy, most effective in raising productively of labour which is very essential for economic development. Use of local raw material, employment of local labour, skilled and unskilled, would create an impact on income levels and pull the region out its backwardness and promote regional balanced development.

Policy to Promote Industries in Backward Regions in India

Though India embarked on developmental planning in 1950 the concern for the disparities in regional development was found, for the first time, in its Industrial Policy Resolution in 1956, which stressed the necessity to reduce disparities in industrial development through faster industrialisation of backward areas. However, little was done during the First and Second Plans. It was the Third Five Year Plan, which strongly drew the attention to the problem of regional disparities. The Third Five Year Plan document contained a special chapter on balanced regional development. It was stated in the Third Plan Summary Document that the development of regions and of the national economy as a whole have to be viewed as part of the same process. The progress of the national economy will be reflected in the rate of growth realised by different regions and in turn greater development of the resources in the regions must contribute towards accelerating the rate of progress in the country as whole.[28] In order to achieve this goal, the third plan suggested the measure which include intensive development of agriculture, extension of irrigation, the programme of village and small industries, the large-scale expansion of power development of road and road transport etc.,

But the steps taken by the Government during the Third Plan Period could not reduce the regional disparities. In fact these disparities became wider which caused anxiety to the Government. The Fourth Five Year Plan (1969-74) admitted. "The social and economic costs of servicing large concentration of population are prohibitive, beyond a certain limit unit costs of providing utilities and services increased rapidly with increase in the size of the cities. In the ultimate analysis problem is that of planning the spatial location of economic activity throughout the country. A beginning must be made by tackling the problems of larger cities and taking positive steps for dispersal through suitable creation of small centres in the rest of the areas.[29]

This concern of the Government about the regional disparities and inequality in income and employment initiated it to take same measures to remove. How to set right the regional imbalances and the planning for development of backward region did start during the Fourth Five Year Plan. During the Fourth Five Year Plan certain changes in distribution of central assistance was introduced which was based on the criteria like population, tax effort, per capita state income requirements of irrigation and power projects etc. District and area plans were also considered essential for ensuring optimal distribution and utilisation of resources to reduce disparities between different areas and segments of population.

In the Fifth Five Year Plan (1974-79) emphasis was put on the development of backward areas through special programmes like hill area development programmes, Integrated Tribal Areas Development programme etc., with a view to redistribute personal income.

In the Sixth Five Year Plan (1980-85) reduction of regional disparities became a parallel objective of Indian Planning, through progressive reduction inequalities and diffusion in technological benefits. Sixth Plan, therefore, stated that "the measures to be pursued for reduction of regional inequalities have to be consistent with the general objective of achieving a SPC growth in the economy as a whole".[30] There was a change in the emphasis on the role of states in implementing the policy in the direction of reducing regional disparities. The Plan emphatically states that backwardness does not recognize state boundaries and it may be necessary over time to take account of this in the policies concerning resource transfer relatively richer stated need to pay adequate attention to the backward areas with in their territories and the claims of backward states must also be sustained for the basis of proven programmes for the benefit of backward regions.[31] This statement clearly indicates the increasing role of the state in the coming years in policy during 6th Plan. It was highly influenced by the recommendation of the National Committee on the backward areas development (Under the Chairmanship of B.Shivaraman) which submitted its report to the Government in 1981.

Criteria for the Identification of Backward Areas

Though successive Five Year Plans placed emphasis on balanced development, it was only in 1968 that concrete action was taken by the Central Government. The National Development Council (NDC) in its meeting held on 12th September, 1968 decided that two working groups should be set up for studying the question of regional imbalances. In pursuance of this decision, two working groups were set up by the planning commission; One for recommending the criteria for the identification of backward areas under the Chairmanship of B.D. Pande and the other for recommending the fiscal and financial incentives for starting industries in the backward areas under the chairmanship of N.N. Wanchoo.

The Pande working Group recommended that the following criteria to be applied in aggregate for the purpose of identification of industrially backward states and Union Territories. (a) Total Per Capital Income, (b) Per Capital Income from industry and mining, (c) Number of workers in registered factories (d) per capita annual consumption of electricity (e) length of surfaced roads in relation to population and the area of the states and (f) railway millage in relation to population and the area of the State.

On the basis of these criterias, the provide group recommended and the Government of India approved that the following industrially backward states and Union Territories should qualify for special treatment by way of incentives for industrial development.

Incentives for Development of Backward Area

The Wanchoo Working Group recommended the following set of fiscal incentives for attracting the entrepreneurs to set up industries in the backward area.[33]

a) Grant of higher development rebate to industries located in Backward areas.

b) Grant of exemption from Income-tax, including Corporate tax for 5 years after providing for the development rebate.

c) Exemption from import duties on plant and machinery component, etc., imported by units set up in backward areas.

d) Exemption from excise duties for a period of five years.

e) Exemption from sales tax, both on raw materials and finished products to units set up in specified backward areas for a period of five years from the date of their going into production and

f) Transport subsidy.

We feel that there is a case for giving transport subsidy to reason for special remoteness of certain areas, for taking out the finished products for a period of 5 years up to 400 miles, the distance should be considered as normal and beyond that the transportation cost for finished products should be subsidised for such backward areas as may be selected in the State of Assam, Nagaland, Manipur, Tripura, NFFA and Andamans. The Transport subsidy should be equivalent to 50 per cent of the cost of transportation in case of backward areas specified in Jammu and Kashmir State.[34]

The Criteria for the selection of the Industrially backward districts in the State and Union Territories were to be decided by the Planning Commission in consultation with the Financial Institutions and the State Government, in the light of the two sets of Criteria recommended by the Pande Committee. The following set of Criteria was evolved by the Planning Commission for the purpose of identification of industrially backward districts to quality for concessional finance.[35]

a) Per capita food grains or commercial crops production depending as whether the district is predominantly a producer of food grains of cash crops.

b) Ratio of agricultural workers to population.

c) Per capita industrial output (gross).

d) Number of factory employees per lakh of population or alternatively number of persons engaged in the secondary and territory activities per lack of population.

e) Length of surfaced roads in relation to population or railway mileage in relation to population.

Identification of Backward Areas

Six Point Formula

With a view to maintaining the integrity of the State against the back ground of certain political unrest in the state, the Government of India announced a six point formula in 1973. In accordance with the Formula the Government of India agreed to make available a special assistance of Rs. 90 crores for the accelerated development of the backward areas in the State during Fifth Plan which, necessitated the identification of backward areas.

After the special Central assistance came to an end by the end of Fifth Plan, the Government of Andhra Pradesh constituted a technical committee to advise the Government on the Criteria to be adopted for the identification of the backward areas in the States and other technical issues related to the problems such as unit of identification etc.,

Identification of Backward Taluks

In conformity with the objective of the National Planning the removal or atleast reduction of regional imbalances in development is an important objective of the Sixth Five Year Plan of Andhra Pradesh. In this context accelerated development of backward areas and target groups assume importance[37] while at the national level, the State could be considered as a unit for assessing the relative levels of development and evolving policies for reducing the disparities between these units, at the State level also there is need to study the existence of disparities with in the State among its regions. Despite the development achieved in various sectors during the past Five Year Plan periods, regional disparities still persist both at National and State levels. In the context of removal of regional imbalances, the identification of backward areas assumes considerable importance, since it is only by a policy of accelerated development of such areas that regional imbalanced can be removed or atleast reduced. In the context, the Planning Department of the Government of Andhra Pradesh had undertaken a number exercises in the past for identifying the backward areas. The first of such exercise in the state was with reference to the identification of drought affected taluks. The committee identified 118 taluks for being eligible to be classified as backward, the region-wise break up the coastal Andhra 35, Rayalaseema, 24 and Telangana.[39]

The Committee, therefore, recommended to the State Government to accept and declare 118 taluks, shown in Appendix as backward for allocating any special funds/assistance for the development of such areas.

Growth of Small-Scale Industries in Andhra Pradesh

The District Industries Centre have been setup in the State of Andhra Pradesh in 3 phases - the first phase with effect from 1-12-1978 covering 11 districts, the second phase from 1-7-1979 covering 3 districts and the third phase from, 1-3-1981 covering the rest of 8 districts. However, the District Industries Centres started for implementing the programmes from April, 1980. Each District Industries Centre was originally conceived to have a staffing pattern of one general manager in the cadre of joint director, supported by 7 functional managers in the cadre of Deputy Director in the disciplines as instructed by the Government of India. Subsequently it has been modified to have 4 functional managers in the disciplines as communicated by the Government of India. According to the restructured used staffing pattern, the State Government have created one post of general manager, supported by 4 functional managers to look after the disciplines economic investigation and infrastructure, credit village industries and training and raw material and marketing. The State Government also sanctioned 10 posts of project managers at each District Industries Centre in the districts of Srikakulam, East Godavari, Krishna, Prakasam, Chittoor, Anantapur, Karimnagar, Nalgonda, medak and Ranga Reddy. The Project managers act as technical specialists in District Industries Centres relevant to the needs of the districts. At the block level, extension officers are working to identify the artisan candidates and entrepreneurs during the credit campaigns and arrange training programmes, electrification in the traders like auto-mechanism, tailoring, mat weaving, matches manufacturing, leather, training, typewriting, radio and T.V. mechanism through various promotional institutions under different schemes, Stipends are provided to the candidates during training, Entrepreneurs are also selected for improvement of skills, talents and managerial abilities through training programmes conducted by the Andhra Pradesh productivity council, Small Industries Service Institute, Small Industries Extension Training Institute (APITCO), Andhra Pradesh Small-Scale Industries Development Corporation (APSSIDC) and State Finance Corporation (SFC).

District-wise Units, Fixed Capital and Employment Before and After Inception of District Industries Centres

The district-wise analysis of small-scale industries units, fixed capital and employment is undertaken to study the variations in the growth of these variables after the inception of DIC. The table shows the details relating to these aspects.

Before inception of District Industries Centres there were 30342 small-scale units functioning in the state. By 1988 the number of units have risen to 65832, showing an increase of 47 per cent. Fixed capital has increased more rapidly from Rs. 150.62 crores to over Rs. 479.44 crores by 218 per cent. Thus, the starting of DICs has produced a positive effect not only on the number of units functioning but also on fixed capital and employment.

District-wise analysis suggested that both before and after the inception of District Industries Centres, there were inter dis-

Table 2.4 : Product-wise Growth of Units, Fixed Capital and Employment

Sl. No.	Industry Group	*Before Inception of DIC (Upto 1979)*			*After Inception of DIC March, 1988*			*Percentage Change*		
		Units	*Fixed Capital (Rs. in Crores)*	*Employment*	*Units*	*Fixed Capital (Rs. in Crores)*	*Employment*	*Units*	*Fixed Capital (Rs. in Crores)*	*Employment*
1.	Food Products	7363	46.27	87755	16773	150.12	153594	228	324	175
2.	Beverages and Tobacco Products	371	3.20	24408	807	7.38	31493	218	231	129
3.	Cotton Textiles	535	6.17	18735	949	15.14	32346	117	245	173
4.	Wool, Silk and Synth Fibre Textiles	42	0.26	499	59	0.54	650	140	208	130
5.	June, Heep and Mesta Products	13	0.10	557	30	0.17	660	231	170	118
6.	Hosiery and Garments	639	1.48	8991	1346	5.70	14552	211	385	162
7.	Wood Products	2514	3.04	16124	5112	10.42	29840	203	264	185
8.	Paper Products and Printing	2347	11.67	17007	4498	31.65	28242	192	271	166
9.	Leather Products	691	1.50	4274	1611	3.65	8733	233	243	204
10.	Rubber and Plastic Products	1027	6.52	9237	2994	31.84	20872	292	488	226

(Contd.)

Table 2.4 : (Contd.)

Sl. No.	Industry Group	Before Inception of DIC (Upto 1979)			After Inception of DIC March, 1988			Percentage Change		
		Units	Fixed Capital (Rs. in Crores)	Employ-ment	Units	Fixed Capital (Rs. in Crores)	Employ-ment	Units	Fixed Capital (Rs. in Crores)	Employ-ment
11.	Chemicals and Chemical Products	1729	13.96	22754	3143	47.15	37641	182	338	165
12.	Non-Meallic Mineral Products	2418	9.28	35716	5348	42.48	79565	221	458	223
13.	Basic Metal Industries	495	8.13	9759	1022	27.58	17565	206	339	180
14.	Metal Products	4368	12.79	32377	7724	28.56	52508	177	223	162
15.	Machinery and Parts except Electrical	2085	11.10	15457	4864	30.45	29876	233	274	193
16.	Electrical Machinery	509	4.39	6753	1451	15.44	14169	285	352	210
17.	Transport Equipment and Parts	438	1.80	3715	801	4.30	6890	183	239	185
18.	Misc. Manufacturing Industries	477	2.05	4292	940	6.78	6891	197	282	161
19.	Repairs and Servicing	2281	6.01	12028	6360	21.09	27756	279	351	231
	Total	**30342**	**150.62**	**330438**	**65832**	**479.45**	**593817**	**217**	**318**	**180**

Source : Government of Andhra Pradesh, Hyderabad, Commissioner of Industries.

trict variations in respect of number of units, fixed capital and employment. Before the inception of District Industries, Centres in 8 districts Vijayawada, East Godavari, West Godavari, Krishana, Guntur, Prakasam, Nellore, Anantapur and Hyderabad, the number of units functioning was above the state average. On the other hand in the districts of Srikakulam, Vijayanagaram, Mahabubnagar, Rangareddy, Medak, Nizambad, Adilabad, Warangal and Nalgonda, the number of units functioning was far below the State average. Similar trend was observed in respect of fixed capital and employment. In seven districts the average fixed capital and average employment were above the state average.

After inception of District Industries Centres, the number of districts above the state average has gone upto nine in the case of units functioning and employment, while in respect of fixed capital the number remained at seven. After the establishment of District Industries Centres, a considerable progress has been achieved in all these respects in all the regions of the state. However, the progress in different regions has been uneven. In coastal Andhra regions through the progress has been uneven the number of units has risen by 116 per cent, while fixed capital and employment have increased by 188 per cent and 78 per cent respectively. The corresponding percentage increases in the number of units fixed capital and employment were 89, 181 and 65 respectively for Rayalaseema and 130, 252 and 80 respectively for Telangana. A study of district - wise shares in total number of units fixed capital and employment in the state before and after the setting up of District Industries Centres will throw light on changes in their shares and policy of the Government towards backward regions. The developed districts are those whose percentage share was above 4.35 in respect of number of units, fixed capital and employment and district whose percentage share is below these are considered to be less developed districts, the tale below shows the details.

The Table shows that after setting up of District Industries Centres there has been an increase in the percentage share with regard to number of units, fixed capital and employment in all the less developed districts with the exception of Anantapur, Chittoor, Cuddapah and Kurnool in Rayalaseema region, nellore in coastal Andhra region and Adilabad in telangana region. In the developed

Table 2.5 : District-wise Percentage of Variation of Small-Scale Industrial Units, Fixed Capital and Employment

Sl. No. Industry Group	Before Inception of DIC (Upto 1979)			After Inception of DIC March, 1988			Percentage Change		
	Units	Fixed Capital (Rs. in Crores)	Employ-ment	Units	Fixed Capital (Rs. in Crores)	Employ-ment	Units	Fixed Capital (Rs. in Crores)	Employ-ment
I. **Coastal Region :**									
1. Srikakulam	1.90	1.19	1.77	3.28	1.93	2.65	+1.38	+0.74	+0.88
2. Vizianagaram	1.40	1.22	1.57	2.77	1.57	2.25	+1.37	+0.35	+0.68
3. Visakhapatnam	3.44	3.21	3.41	5.12	3.54	4.49	+1.68	+0.13	+1.08
4. East Godavari	6.45	5.45	6.03	5.98	5.00	5.96	–0.47	–0.45	–0.07
5. West Godavari	5.40	4.54	6.03	4.97	4.43	5.30	–0.43	–0.01	–0.73
6. Krishna	9.49	8.56	7.40	7.54	6.72	6.64	–1.85	–1.84	–0.76
7. Guntur	6.42	6.72	9.43	5.53	4.92	8.28	0.89	–1.80	–1.15
8. Prakasam	4.62	2.60	4.82	4.66	2.02	5.18	+0.04	+0.22	+0.36
9. Nellore	5.65	4.05	2.23	4.58	2.98	3.56	–1.07	–1.07	–0.67
Total	**44.77**	**37.54**	**44.67**	**44.53**	**33.91**	**44.31**	**–0.24**	**–3.62**	**–0.36**
II. **Rayalaseema Region**									
10. Chittoor	4.16	2.72	2.90	3.36	3.57	2.88	–0.80	+0.85	–0.02
11. Cuddapah	3.87	3.79	3.49	3.83	2.53	3.08	–0.01	–1.26	–0.41
12. Anantapur	4.43	3.40	3.61	3.49	2.66	3.06	–0.94	–0.74	–0.55
13. Kurnool	3.44	3.32	3.65	3.16	2.91	3.50	–0.28	–0.42	–0.15
Total	**15.90**	**13.23**	**13.67**	**13.84**	**11.67**	**12.52**	**–0.26**	**–1.57**	**–1.15**

(Contd.)

Table 2.5 : (Contd.)

Sl. No.	Industry Group	Before Inception of DIC (Upto 1979)			After Inception of DIC March, 1988			Percentage Change		
		Units	Fixed Capital (Rs. in Crores)	Employment	Units	Fixed Capital (Rs. in Crores)	Employment	Units	Fixed Capital (Rs. in Crores)	Employment
III.	**Telengana Region**									
14.	Mahaboob Nagar	2.35	1.86	1.34	2.92	3.55	1.93	+0.67	+1.69	+0.59
15.	Ranga Reddy	2.92	7.56	4.21	5.73	14.05	7.57	+2.81	+6.49	+3.36
16.	Hyderabad	16.04	22.04	16.57	11.09	10.62	12.11	–4.95	–11.42	–4.46
17.	Medak	3.02	4.99	3.93	3.53	9.43	4.78	–1.51	+4.44	+0.85
18.	Nizamabad	2.29	2.38	4.43	2.88	2.24	3.98	+0.59	–0.14	–0.45
19.	Adilabad	1.59	2.14	2.84	1.54	1.57	2.12	–0.05	0.57	0.72
20.	Karimnagar	1.34	1.91	2.18	3.72	3.21	2.63	0.38	+1.30	+0.45
21.	Warangal	2.60	1.83	2.03	3.02	2.97	2.62	0.42	+1.14	+0.59
22.	Khammam	3.35	2.20	1.84	3.75	2.58	2.43	0.40	+0.38	+0.59
23.	Nalgonda	2.93	2.32	2.29	3.45	4.20	3.00	0.52	+1.88	+0.61
	Total	**39.33**	**49.23**	**41.66**	**41.63**	**54 .42**	**43.17**	**2.30**	**+5.19**	**+1.51**
	Andhra Pradesh	**100.00**	**100.00**	**100.00**	**100.00**	**100.00**	**100.00**			

Source : Government of Andhra Pradesh, Hyderabad, Commissioner of Industries.

districts the percentage share in respect of units, fixed capital and employment has declined after inception of DICs, exception being the districts of Range Reddy and Medak districts where the shares have substantially improved. This may perhaps be due to the proximity of the districts to Hyderabad where all facilities provided by the promotional institutions are available.

Product-Wise Growth of Units, Fixed Capital and Employment after Inception of District Industries Centres

Product-wise analysis of the growth of units, fixed capital and employment will be useful in the study of the effects of District Industries Centres in different categories of industries. The details relating to these aspects are shown in the table.

The table shows that there was more than a one fold increase in most of the categories of industries after inception of District industries Centres, in number of units and fixed capital and about two fold increase in the case of employment the growth was substantially higher in rubber and plastic products, non metallic mineral products, wool - silk and synthetic fibre textiles and jute, hemp and mesta products. It shows that with a period of a title over 8 years after the District Industries Centres have set up there was a rapid growth in a terms of units, fixed capital and employment.

Conclusion

The performance of District Industries Centres in the State of Andhra Pradesh is relatively better when compared to that of District Industries Centres in the country as a whole. However, inter and intra-district variations continue to exist even after the setting up of District Industries Centers in the state, even though the concentration of units, fixed capital and employment has declined to some extent in recent times. Further, the small-scale industries units in the state are confronting certain problems, some with the purview of District Industries Centres and others beyond their control. Unless the lapses with in and outside District Industries Centres are eliminated the very objective of establishing District Industries Centres in state will be defeated.

Union Territories

All Union Territories except Chandigarh, Delhi and Pondicherry.

Table 2.6 : District-wise Units, Fixed Capital and Employment

Sl. No. Industry Group	*Before Inception of DIC (Upto 1979)*			*After Inception of DIC March, 1988*			*Percentage Change*		
	Units	*Fixed Capital (Rs. 000')*	*Employment*	*Units*	*Fixed Capital (Rs. 000')*	*Employment*	*Units*	*Investment*	*Employment*
I. <u>Coastal Region :</u>									
1. Srikakulam	575	17695	5845	2157	92798	15759	275	415	170
2. Vizianagaram	426	18417	5170	1823	74922	13310	328	307	157
3. Visakhapatnam	1044	48291	11264	3373	170015	26667	223	252	137
4. East Godavari	1958	82079	19920	3934	239769	35380	101	192	78
5. West Godavari	1640	68363	19919	3271	212311	31454	100	211	58
6. Krishna	2881	128953	24461	5034	322393	39439	75	150	61
7. Guntur	1947	101272	31159	3641	235848	49171	87	133	58
8. Prakasam	1403	39121	15922	3070	135337	30782	119	246	93
9. Nellore	1713	61056	13986	3014	142659	21161	76	134	51
Total	**13587**	**165447**	**147646**	**29317**	**1626052**	**263123**	**116**	**188**	**78**
II. <u>Rayalaseema Region</u>									
10. Chittoor	1262	40925	9582	2210	171139	17034	75	318	78
11. Cuddapah	1173	57051	11542	2521	121205	18036	115	113	59
12. Anantapur	1344	51241	11976	2298	127502	18191	71	149	52
13. Kurnool	1044	50008	12062	2080	139237	20789	99	178	72
Total	**4823**	**199225**	**45162**	**9109**	**59083**	**74320**	**89**	**181**	**65**

(Contd.)

Table 2.6 : (Contd.)

Sl. No. Industry Group	Before Inception of DIC (Upto 1979)			After Inception of DIC March, 1988			Percentage Change		
	Units	Fixed Capital (Rs. 000')	Employ-ment	Units	Fixed Capital (Rs. 000')	Employ-ment	Units	Ivest-ment	Employ-ment
III. <u>Telengana Region</u>									
14. Mahaboob Nagar	683	28052	4437	1920	170285	11461	81	507	158
15. Ranga Reddy	885	113819	13910	3776	673525	44962	327	492	223
16. Hyderabad	4866	331968	54753	7301	509573	71932	50	54	31
17. Medak	613	75219	12994	2322	452174	28414	279	501	119
18. Nizamabad	695	35885	14654	1895	106977	23644	173	198	61
19. Adilabad	481	32190	9392	1016	74100	12599	111	133	34
20. Karimnagar	1014	28775	7199	2449	154108	15608	142	436	117
21. Warangal	788	27557	6696	1991	142427	15487	152	417	131
22. Khammam	1017	33187	6075	2468	123502	14446	143	172	138
23. Nalgonda	890	34900	7580	2268	201546	17281	155	477	135
Total	**11932**	**741552**	**137690**	**27406**	**2609217**	**256374**	**130**	**252**	**86**
Andhra Pradesh	**30342**	**1506224**	**330498**	**65832**	**4794352**	**593817**	**117**	**218**	**80**
X	**1319**	**65488**	**14370**	**2862**	**208450**	**25818**			

Source : Government of Andhra Pradesh, Hyderabad, Commissioner of Industries.

Subsequently, Meghalaya, Himachal Pradesh and Sikkim and the Union Territory of Pondicherry were added to the above list. The Pande Group also recommended the following criteria or indicators of backwardness, for identification of backward districts in backward states. Union Territories.

(a) District should be outside a radius of about 50 miles from larger cities and large industrial projects.

(b) Poverty of the people as indicated by low per capita income starting from the lowest to 25% below the state average.

(c) High density of population in relation to utilisation of productive resources and employment opportunities as indicated by

  (i) Low percentage of population engaged in secondary and territory activities (25% below the state average may be considered as backward.

  (ii) Low percentage of factory employment (25% below the state average may be considered as backward.

  (iii) Now or under utilisation of economic and natural resources like minerals, forests etc.,

  (iv) Adequate availability of electric power of likelihood of its availability with in the next one or two years.

  (v) Availability transport and communication facilities or likelihood of their availability within the next cn or two years, and

  (vi) Adequate availability of water or likelihood of its availability with in the one or two years. The Pande Group felt that about 20 to 30 districts in all may be finally selected for grant of special incentives during the Fourth Plan Period. The group had suggested that such districts should have a potential for development so that efforts could be concentrated on these selected districts in the first instance, and gradually extended to all the remaining districts.

Table 2.7 : Industry Backward Districts; State-wise Summary

State/Union	*Percentage of Total Area of the State*	*Backward District*	*Total Population of the State*
Developed (A)			
West Bengal	13	82	68
Tamil Nadu	8	64	60
Gujarat	10	67	49
Maharashtra	13	54	42
Punjab	4	39	35
Haryana	4	30	39
Karnataka	11	67	63
Kerala	5	42	52
Total A			
Backward (B)			
Andhra Pradesh	14	72	59
Bihar	9	47	55
Rajasthan	16	62	54
Madhya Pradesh	36	87	83
Assam	7	78	76
Uttar Pradesh	37	68	62
Orissa	8	61	48
Jammu & Kashmir	10	100	100
Nagaland	3	100	100
Himachal Pradesh	7	88	73
Manipur	5	100	100
Meghalaya	2	100	100
Tripura	3	100	100
Goa, Daman & Diu	3	100	
Pondicherry	4	100	
Andaman & Nicobar Islands	1	100	
Arunachal Pradesh	5	100	
Dadra & Nagar Haveli	1	100	
Lakshadeep	1	69	
Mizoram			
Total (B)		71	58

All India : the number of districts declained has sencerisen to 247.

Source : Ministry of Industrial Development, Guidelines for Industry 1984–85, June, 84.

Appendix

1. (a) Accelerated development of the backward areas of the State. Planned Development of State Capital with special resources remarked for these purposes.

   (b) Association of representatives of such backward areas with experts in the formulation of development schemes.

   (c) Constitution of a State Level Planning Board and sub-committees for different backward areas.

2. (a) Preference to local candidates in the matter of admission to educational institutions.

   (b) Establishment of a new Central University at Hyderabad to augment the existing educational facilities.

3. Local candidates given preference in the matter of direct recruitment to

   a) Non-Gazetted Posts (Other than those in the secretariat under Heads of Departments and in the State Level Officers Hyderabad City Police).

   b) Corresponding posts under the local bodies.

   c) The posts of Tehsildars, Junior Engineers and Civil Assistance Surgeons.

4. Constitution of a high power Administrative Tribunal to deal with the grievances of the services in matters of appointment seniority, promotion etc. This would limit resource to the judiciary.

5. Necessary Constitutional amendments be enhanced to avoid litigations and uncertainty.

6. Abolition of Multi Rules and Regional Committees:

A. Coastal Region

1. **Vishakhapatnam District :**

   Anakapalli, Yellamanchli, Gajapathinagaram, Narsipatnam, Chodavaram, Samarlakota, Bheemunipatnam, Vizianagaram, Chintapalli, Paderu, Vishkhapatnam.

2. **East Godavari District:**

   Yellavaram, Peddarum, Prathipadu, Tuni, Pithapuram.

3. **West Godavari District:**

Polavaram, Chintalapudi.

4. **Krishna District:**

Nandigama, jaggayapeta, Tiruvuru, Backward Talugs (next page), Nuzivedu.

5. **Guntur District:**

Vinukonda, Palnadu, Sattenpalli.

6. **Nellore District:**

Gudur, Sullurpet, Venkatagiri, Rapur, Atmakur, Udayagiri, Kavali.

7. **Prakasam District:**

Ongole, Kandukuru, Kanigiri, Padili, Darsi, Addanki, markapur, Giddalpur.

B. Rayalaseema Region:

1. **Chittoor District:**

Palemaneru, Kuppam, panganur, Madanapalli, Vayalpad, Satyavedu, Chittoor, banaganipalli, Srikalashsti, Puttur, (Pulivendula, Kamalapuram).

2. **Cuddapah District:**

Rayachoti, Jammalamadugu, Badwel.

3 **Anantapur District:**

Kalyandurg, Urvakonda, Rayadurg, Dharmavaram, Kadiri, Penukonda, Hindupur, Madakasira.

4. **Kurnool District:**

Nandikotkur, Atmakur, Allagadda, Koilkuntla, Pattikonda, Alur, Adoni, Kurnool.

C. Telangana Region:

1. **Mahaboob Nagar District:**

Achampet, Kollapur Nagar, Kurnool, Wanaparthi, Alampur, Gadwal, Makthal, Atmakur, Kadangal.

2. **Hyderabad District:**

Ibrahimpatnam, Chevelli, Parti, Tandur, Vikarabad, medchal.

3. **Medak District:**

   Sanga Redy, Narayana, Adndole, Gadwal, Siddipet.

4. **Nizambad District:**

   Yellareddi, Madnoor, Banswada.

5. **Adilabad District:**

   Adilabad, Asifabad, Sirpur, Chennur, Luneetipet, Khananapur, Boath, Mudhole, Nirmal.

6. **Karmnagar District:**

   Metpalle, Jagtial, Peddapalle, karimnagar, Sicilla, Manthani, Huzurabad.

7. **Warangal District :**

   Warangal, Parkal, Mulugu, Narasampet, Mahaboobad, Jangoon.

8. **Khammam District:**

   Madhera

9. **Nalgonda District:**

   Ramannapet, Bhongir, Devarakonda, Suryapet

List of 118 Talugu Identified as Backward

a) Coastal Region:

Srikakular:

Narasannapeta, Salur, Bobbili, Palthapatnam, Parvathipuram, Palkonda, Chepurapally.

Visakhapatnam,:

Ellamanchali, Bheemunipatanam, Chodavaram, S.Kota, Narsipatnam, Gajapathjinagaram, Chintapally Panderu.

East Godavari:

Chitalapudi, Polavaram.

Krishna:

Tiruruvu, Nandigamma, kaikalur.

Guntur:

Sattenapalle, Palnad, Vinukonda.

Kurnool:

Dhone, Nandikottur, Allgadda, Koilakuntala, Pattikonda, Alur.

Medak:

Meadak, Zaheerabad, Gajwal, Narsapur, Andole, Narayanakhed, Siddipet.

Mahaboob Nagar:

Shadnagar, Gawal, nagarkurnool, Kedangal, kalvakurthy, Achampet, Alampur, Killapur, Wargrarthy, Atmakur.

Nalgonda:

Huzurnagar, nalgonda, Miryalaguda, Ramampet, Suryapet, Devarakonda.

Warangal:

Mahaboodbad, Farigaon, Mulug, Parkal, narampet.

Khammam:

Madhikera, Seltupalli, Yellanudu, burgampadu, Bhadrachalam, Nugur.

Karimnagar:

Peddapalli, Sirsilla, Huzurbad, Jagitial, Manthani, Adilabad, Lakethipet, Nirmal, Asifbad, Khanpur, Sirpur, Mudhole, Adilabad, Chinur, Boathutuon.

References:

1. United Nations Organisation, Report on the Process and Problems of Industrialisation in underdeveloped countries (New York) United nations, 1955) p. 16.
2. Gunnar Myrdal, *An International Economy* (New York: Harper & Brothers, 1956) p.226.
3. *Ibid.*, p. 226.
4. C. Ganguli, *Studies in Indian Economic Problems* (Calcutta, 1978) p.1.
5. National Institute of Small Industry Extension Training Industrial Policy Resolution, 1980 (Hyderabad, NISIET, 1980) p.2.
6. *Ibid.*, p.8.
7. Government of India, the *First Five Year Plan - A Draft outline* (New Delhi: Planning Commission, 1951) p. 162.
8. Government of India, *Second Five Year Plan* (New Delhi, Planning Commission, 1956) p. 429.
9. Government of India, *Third Five Year Plan* (New Delhi, Planning Commission, 1960) P. 426.
10. Government of India, *Fourth Five Year Plan* (New Delhi; Planing Commission, 1970), p. 284.
11. Government of India, *Draft Fifth Five Year Plan 1974-79* volume II (New Delhi; Planning Commission, 1974) p. 160.
12. Government of India, *Sixth Five Year Plan 1980-85* (New Delhi, Planning Commission, 1980) p. 186.
13. State Bank of India (1988), *Seventh Five Year Plan* (1985-90), Monthly Review June, p. 308.
14. *Ibid.*, p. 309.
15. "Eight Plan Proposals" (1990) *Economic Times Daily 31st December, pp.1.*
16. Government of India, Report of the Vilage and Small-Scale Industries Committee, *Second Five Year Plan*, New Delhi, Planning Commission, October, 1955, p.6.
17. Alexander, P.C. *Industrial Estate in India*", Bombay Asia Publishing House, 1963 p.

18. Government of India, Report of the working group on Identification of Backward Areas (Pande working Group Report), Planning Commission.

19. Government of India, Report of working Group of Fiscal and Financial Incentives for starting industres in Backward Areas (Report of Wanchoo working Group: Development Commissioner, SSI, Ministry of Industrial Development).

20. Ram, K. Vepa, *Rural Industrial Development*, Development Commissioner, SSI, New Delhi, p. 246.

21. *Small, Industry - The Challenge of the Eighties*, New Delhi, Vikas Publishing House Pvt. Ltd., 1983, p. 60.

22. Sutclifee R.B. *Industry and under development* Addisas Wesley Publishing Co. London 91971) p. 3.

23. Barn P.A., *Political Economy of Growth*, New York (1962) p. 277.

24. Colnean D and Ninon P.F. *Economic of changes in less developed countries* Philip Allan publisher Ltd., Oxford (1978) p. 180.

25. UNIDO *Industrial Development Strategy* Reprinted in (Geralad M. Meier and edited) Leadiong issues in Economic Development (3rd edition) Oxford University Press, York York (1976) p. 659.

26. Rosentein Radan P.N. *Problems of Industrialisation of Eastern and South Eastern Europe Economic Journal* (June-Sep. (1943).

27. *Third Five Year Plan* - Summary Planning Commission, Government of India, p. 47.

28. *Fourth Five Year Plan*; 69-74, Planning Commission, Government of India, p. 399.

29. *Sixth Five Year Plan 80-85* Planning Commission, Government of India, p. 86.

30. *Ibid*, p. 87.

31. Government of India, Report of the working Group on the Identification of Backward Area, Planning Commission, New Delhi, 1965, Page, 5.

32. Government of India, *Fiscal and Financial Incentives for starting Industries in Backward Areas*, Development Commissioner (S.S.I.), New Delhi, 1969 p. 2-3.
33. Government of India, *Fiscal and Financhal Incentries for starting Industries in Backward Areas* Development Commissioner, (SSI) New Delhi, 1969, pp. 16-17.
34. Government of India, Report on Industrial Disperseal, National Committee on the Development of Backward areas, Planning Commission, New Delhi, October, 1980, p. 12.
35. See Apendix for six points Formula and Appendix 2 for the Taluqs declained backward in different districts under six point formula.
36. Government of A.P., *Sixth Five Year Plan 1980-85*, A.P. Department of Planning and Cooperation, Hyderabad-1980, p. 234.
37. Government of Andhra Pradesh, Report a Technical Committee on Identification of Backward Areas in Andhra Pradesh. Finance and Planning Department, Hyderabad 1981, pp 2-6.

3

Industrial Economy

Introduction

Establishment of District Industries Centres (DIC's) In 1978 is an importance milestone to stimulate the development of small industries in the district concerned. The District Industries Centres prepared action plan for five years by taking into account different industries which are feasible and viable, the demand for various products and resources, which are available in the area, region concerned.This information which is useful for selection of the location of the unit and also the selection of the product to be manufactured in that area/region, is provided to the entrepreneurs. District Industries Centres also provides consultancy and technical guidance for setting up of industries in the district. Further, it assists the entrepreneurs in getting credit from financial institutions, supply of scarce raw materials from raw materials servicing centres, marketing facilities under the scheme of hire purchase.[1] Besides, to improve the entrepreneurial talents and skills, it imparts training through various institutions.[2] The scheme "Self-Employment for educated unemployed Youth" (in A.P., it is Gramodya) has been implemented by the District Industries Centres as a nodal agency. This scheme aims at encouraging the educated unemployed persons in the age group of 18 to 35 years to undertake self-employment ventures in the field of industry, servicing and business activities. The identified beneficiaries are entitled to get the composite loan upto Rs. 25,000 to Rs. 35,000 in the case of industry has it has been reduced to Rs. 15,000 in the case of business. In the case of servicing units the loan amount remained unaltered. The loan amount is provided by the banks after the selection is made by the District Industries Centre task force.[3]

Small-Scale Sector occupies an important place in Industrial Economy of the world. It is a misconception that small-scale or medium size enterprises are meant only for developing or under developed economy. Even in the highly developed countries of Western Europe, the U.S. and Japan, the total number of small firms make up the overwhelming majority of all business enterprises. It is true that because of their limited size, they have far less impact on the statistics for national output, investment and employment. In developing economics, small-scale industries are specially important in the context of employment opportunities, equitable distribution of wealth, balanced regional growth and above all, the preservation and development of ancient art and craft.

Small-Scale sector is widespread throughout industrial world due to certain common factors. Stately and Morse have suggested a categorization of those industries in which small-scale industries are common. The viability of small-scale industries is produced by (a) Location (b) process and (c) market Industries based on disperesed raw materials, the products which are sold locally and have high transfer costs and the service industries are profitability operated in small-scale sector due to locational influences.

The market influences, particularly in case of differentiated products having low scale economic industries serving small local markets also promote small-scale operations.

District Industries Centre

An important Institution setup at the District level for industrial promotion is the District Industries Centres (DIC). It is major structural innovation introduction in May, 1978 to serve as a unified agency for providing all the services and support required by small and village industries under a single roof. Compared to the earlier pattern of District Industries Officer/Assistant Director of Industries, the institution has been upgraded and headed by a senior person designated as General Manager. He is of the rank of Joint Director of Industries and in certain cases Deputy Director of Industries. There are in all 397 District Industries Centres in the country covering 410 districts. With a senior officer posted at the district level, power have been delegated to him in a number of areas as many organisational innovations are either introduced or contemplated in various states to provide a wide range of services and support to entrepreneurs and artisans.

The General Manager has four functional managers concerned with the functional areas of economic investigation, village industries credit, marketing/infrastructure/raw materials. It is planned to augment the strength of functions managers with three project managers specialised in different product groups, based on the needs of a particular district.

It is hopped that the team will be able to give area orientation and project orientation to its activities simultaneously for helping entrepreneurs in various ways. In many States, sub divisional set up has come into being with an assistant director of industries and an Industrial Promotion Officer posted at the sub-divisional headquarters. In addition, at the block level, an Extension Officer (Industries) is in position. In some states, he looks after two to three blocks. It is hoped that an Extention Officer will be given the jurisdiction of not more than one block in the near future, to cope with a number of development schemes for which he is held responsible as a field level functionary. Strong district and lower level teams are an important aspect of industrial administration in the country.

The objectives of the development programmes for the small and village industries in the Fourth Plan were capacity utilisation and improvement of the quality of production techniques so as to enable them to produce quality goods. In order to protect the small industries from large industries, the existing reservations were to be continued and the list of items for exclusive production of small industries were to be enlarged. It also laid emphasis on decentralization and dispersal of industries and promotion of agro based industries. After recognising the ineffectiveness of the licensing policy to control the concentration of industries, the Government has stressed the dispersal of industries to backward areas by providing capital investment, subsidy, transport subsidy, income tax concession, concessional finance, scarce raw materials and machinery at concessional rate of interest. Further State Governments have also provided several incentives, such as power concession, sales tax concession and other facilities to promote these industries in order to achieve the balanced regional development.

Provision of all these facilities has resulted in spectacular growth of village and small industries sector accounted for about 40 per cent in the entire industrial production and this resulted in a generation of more employment opportunities. However, the additional employment generated by these industries has not kept pace with the population explosion resulting at the beginning of the First Plan (1951) to more than 20 million up to the end of Fifth Plan.

The Main Objectives

The District Industries Centres programme has been launched through out the country to help in effective development of small, tiny and cottage industries all over the country including rural and backward areas. The main objective of the programme is to provide a package of assistance needed for setting up small, cottage any tiny industries with greater emphasis on maximum generation of employment. 422 District Industries Centres have been established all over the country covering all the districts except the four metropolitan cities of Bombay, Delhi, Madras and Calcutta. They provide requisite service and support, assistance to the entrepreneurial in the forms of technical guidance, project reports and assistance in getting the credit and other essential inputs.

Implementation of DIC Programme

In accordance with the instructions of the Union Government, the Government of Andhra Pradesh agreed to set up DIC's in all the district headquarters of the state within two years commencing from 1978.

In G.O.Ms. No. 761, Industries and Commerce (SSI) Department, dt. 3rd October, 1978 the Government of Andhra Pradesh accorded sanction for the establishment of DIC's in eleven districts of Andhra Pradesh out of 22 districts in the state in the first instance viz., 1. Sikakulam, 2. Guntur, 3. Anantapur, 4. Cuddapah, 5. Nalgonda, 6. Khamman, 7. Karimnagar, 8. Vishakhapatnam, 9. Chittoor, 10. Medak and 11. Hyderabad. Thus Anantapur District is one of the eleven districts in Andhra Pradesh where DIC programmes were first launched with effect from 1.11.1978.

Functions of DIC

The G.O. cited specifies the functions of DIC. The following are the functions of the DIC.

1. To survey existing, traditional and new industries and raw materials and human resources, to identify schemes and make market forcaste for different items, to prepare sample techno economic facility reports and offer investment advice to entrepreneurs.
2. To assess the machinery and equipment requirements of small scale, tiny and village and industries, indicate the locations where machinery and equipment for different plants may be available for entrepreneurs to liaison with research institutions and arrange for the supply of machinery on hire purchase basis.
3. To arrange for training entrepreneurs of small and tiny units and liaison with small industries service institute, small industries extension training centre and other institutions to keep abreast of research and development in selected product lines and quality methods.
4. To ascertain the raw materials requirements of various units, their sources and prices and to arrange for their bulk purchases for and distribution to entrepreneurs.
5. To maintain liaison with lead banks and other financial institutions, appraise applications, monitor the flow of industrial credit in the district and arrange for financial assistance to entrepreneurs.
6. To organise marketing outlet, maintain liaison with Government procurement agencies, provide market intelligence to entrepreurs, organise market surveys and market development programmes.
7. To give particular attention to the development of Khadi, village and other cottage industries, to maintain liaison with the State Khadi board and organise training programmes for rural artisans.

8. To provide immediate requirements by entrepreneurs in respect of power supply, licences required under Municipal Health and Factories Act for establishment of Industries.
9. To assist entrepreneurs in allotment of worksheds or sites required for establishment of industries in industrial estates.
10. To help in arranging cent per cent loans to educated unemployed belonging to scheduled castes, scheduled tribes and society or economically backward communities for starting industries under special employment scheme.
11. To help in extending suitable technical, training to rural youth to pursue self-employment scheme.
12. To assist entrepreneurs of small units in establishing industries collectively by formation of industries co-operatives.
13. To assist in arranging grant of central and State Government concession and interest, free sabs tax loans to provide capital for purchase of plant and machinery, construction of buildings and allotment of sites to new industrialists.
14. To arrange for the issue of guarantee deeds to new industries in respect of supply of electricity at 25 per cent rebate.

Administrative Framework of DIC

The DIC was conceived to achieve the objective of effective promotion of cottage small industries videly dispersed in rural areas and small towns. To accomplish this task, it was felt, a new administrative frame work was essential, which could, to a large extent, cut across the procedural delays involved in setting up of a new industry. The DIC was, therefore, though of as on administrative device to provide a frame work for implementing the new policy measures.

In the DIC's a critical mass of personnel and facilities are being provided which could spark off a significant growth of industries in the district. The general staffing pattern of the DIC is to have eight core functionaries including a General Manager, leading team of seven functional Deputy Directors of Industries dealing with economic investments, raw materials, machinery and equipment research, extension and training, credit, marketing and cottage industries.[4] The eight functionaries form the nucleus of a team which wanted ultimately draw to itself other personnel working in various promotional agencies both Central and State. Great emphasis has been laid as manning the DIC's with personnel of proved ability and adequate experience having quality of leadership, organisational ability and executive capability.[5] Accordingly the State Government have been advised that wherever adequate number of suitable persons from the existing agencies and departments could not be identified, recruitment may be thrown open to such person from open market.

District Advisory Committee

For an effective co-ordination between the District Industries Centre and other State Government Departments and undertaking local bodies and non-official agencies in the district. The State Government was instructed to constitute a District Advisory Committee headed by the Collector of the District and consisting of district level officers of other Departments and Semi-Government local bodies such as the State Electricity Boards/municipal Chairman/President, District Panchayat President, District Development Officer. This Committee also includes members of legislative Assembly of the district, who would be nominated by Government. Presently, the General Manager of DIC is the convenor of the District Advisory Committee. The District Advisory Committee may meet once in a month or once in two months. However, the Collector may co opt such other officers or non-officials as be feels succesary for the successful working of the DIC.[6] The Committee will approve the action plan prepared by the DIC and review the implementation of various schemes under the DIC programme and the progress is establishment of small and village industries, artisan development programmes and periodically suggests measures for improving the performance.

State Level Committee

To supervise and monitor the activities of DIC's State Government constitutes a State Level Co-ordination Committees, with Minister of Industries as Chairman and the Chief Secretary, the industries Secretary, the Director of Industries, Secretaries in charge of Agriculture, Rural Development and Energy the Development Commissioner in charge of Panchayat Raj Institutions, and the Director, SISI as members. The co-ordination committee meets once in six months to review that activities of the District Indus-

Table 3.1

Sl. No.	Category of Industries	Total	Place of Concentration	Fixed Investment Rs. in lakhs	Employ-ment	Produc-tion Rs. in lakhs
1.	Agro	1093	Kadiri, Anantapur Dharmavaram, Rayadurg	773.75	6018	650.00
2.	Engineering	822	Guntakal, Hindupur	622.08	3817	180.00
3.	Forest	307	Penukonda, Kadiri Tadpatri, Anantapur	103.70	1877	150.00
4.	Mineral	301	Tadpatri, Yadiki, Gooty	592.64	3345	450.00
5.	Textile	391	Hindupur, Dharmavaram, Tadpatri, Raydurg, Kadiri	304.41	4502	200.00
6.	Chemical	153	Tadpatri, Gooty, Anantapur	239.52	2243	150.00
7.	Miscellaneous	352	All Mandals	260.74	1333	150.00

Source : District Industries centre, Anantapur Action Plan.

tries Centres and reports to the Government of India as to their progress, the problems countered and the solutions identified.

Location

Anantapur District is a potential District for Industrial investment. It is famous for Lepakshi Temple and Penukonda Rock Fort of Hamp Vijayanagar fame, Diamond and Gold deposits at Vajrakarur and Ramagiri respectively and the Holy Prasanthi Nilayam of Sri Sathya Sai Baba at Puttaparthi is at the Southern boundary of Andhra Pradesh bordering karnataka State South and West and Kurnool and Cuddapah Districts on its North and Eastern sides and Chittoor District on Southern side. The District has the distinction of having two Universities besides a number of Colleges affiliated to Sri Krishnadevaraya and the Jawahar Lal Nehru Technological Universities.

Hindupur, just 100 km from Bangalore, is on the threshold of developing into a large industrial complex spreading over 600 hectares. Tadipatri has very promosing potential for mineral baed industries. Other potential centres for industry location are Anantapur, Guntakal, Gooty, Dharmavaram, Madakasira, Rayadurg and Kadiri.

Area and Population

Anantapur District has an area of 19134 square kilometers. The district has a population of 25.48 lakhs which accounts for 5.9 per cent of the total area of A.P. 2750.68 (1981 Census) and accounts for 4.75 per cent of the total population of Andhra Pradesh (535.50 lakhs). The density of population of the District is 133 per (There are 964, villages in the District) Sq. Km. The District takes second place in Rayalaseema region with reference to density of population and number of towns and tops in geographcial area. The population of rural and urban to the total population of the District works out to 79.2% and 22.8% in 1991 census as against 82% and 18% of 1971.

The working force in the total population of District forms 42.66% while 57.3 per cent are non workers as per 1991 census out of which 32.40% are in the Agriculture sector, 10.3 per cent other workers. The pattern of distribution of workers to the total population is almost similar in all other districts of Rayalaseema region. The scheduled caste and scheduled tribe population form

13.68% and 3.21% respectively to the total population in the District.

Literacy

The literacy rate is 7.39 (1981 Census):

Administration

The District has been divided into three Revenue Divisions i.e. Anantapur, Dharmavaram and Penukonda and 63 Revenue Mandals and Panchayat Raj Mandals with identical jurisdiction which are the basic administrative and development units. The District has 11 town and 964 Revenue Village of which 28 are unihabited.

Climate

The climate of the District is hot and dry in summer, hot and humid in rainy season and dry in winter, with the temperature varying from 16°C in December-January to 44°C March - May. The District can be categorized as the driest part of Andhra Pradesh.

Rain Fall

The District's normal rainfall is 308 mm and 147 mm during South-West and North-East Monsoon periods respectively.

Table 3.2 : Season-wise Rain-fall

(Rainfall in mms)

Sl. No.	*Item*	*Normal*	*District % to total*
1.	South-west Monsoon	310.8	57.13
2.	North-East Monsoon	147.0	27.02
3.	Winter Period	8.4	1.5
4.	Hot Weather period	77.8	14.3
	Total	**544.0**	**100.00**

Source : Chief Planning Office, Anantapur.

The incidence of rainfall is not uniform of certain therefore the district is frequently prone to drought conditions.

Rain Fall

There are no perennial rivers flowing in the District the Chief river is the Pennar. The Chitravathi is another river. The Hagari river, Chinna Hagari River, Apart from these, streams Pandameru and Madaleru are the other sources of water to various large and small irrigation tanks of this district. The above said rivers and streams flow only during the rain season.

Soils

The major portion of the district is covered with red and black Cotton soil constituting 76 and 24 per cent of the total area of the District respectively. The black cotton soil is found on the Northern part of the District.

Anantapur District is Predominantly agriculture oriented with 68.9% of the work force engaged in

Table 3.3 : Distribution of Work Force in Anantapur District (1991) Census

Sl. No.	Category	Total No. Persons	% total main workers
1.	Cultivators	4,38,044	10.43
2.	Agricultural Labourers	3,88,391	22.00
3.	Marginal Workers	10,87,003	42.7
4.	Total Non-workers	14,61,009	57.3

Source : Hand Book of Statistics, Anantapur District 1990–91.

Forests

The area under forests is 2.13 lakh acres constituting 11 per cent of the total geographical area. The main forest wealth consists of the Beedi leaves, Tangedu Bark, Tamarind, Custard apple fruits and Soapnuts. Another important resource is agavė (Sisal) plant

Table 3.4 : Forest Products and their Income in Anantapur District (1989–90)

Sl.No.	Name of the Material	Rupees
1.	Timber	10,100
2.	Fuel	67,364
3.	Bamboo	——
4.	Other Forest Products including Beedi Leaves	4,01,325
5.	Miscellaneous	9,77,803
	Total	**14,56,592**

Source : District Forest Office, Anantapur.

which is a wild growth. There are organised plantations in Penukonda and Samandepalli Mandals.

Salient Features of Agricultures

The economy of Anantapur District is predominantly agriculture oriented. 205302 acres of land is covered under Paddy cultivation, yielding about 4.00 lakhs MTs. under both Kharif and Rabi seasons. Groundnut is the main commercial crop grown on dry land is mostly rainfed. The total yield per annum is estimated at 4.5 lakhs Mts. Sugar cane cotton and Pulses are the other commercial crops.

Table 3.5 :

Sl. No.	*Item*	*Extent Hectares*	*Yield Lakhs MTs.*
1.	Paddy	60,704	2.00
2.	Groundnut	5,45,000	5.60
3.	Cotton	6,000	4,000.00
4.	Sugarcane	N.A.	14,000.00
5.	Jowar	71,000	58,000.00
6.	Bajra	26,000	16,000.00
7.	Ragi	15,000	27,000.00

Infrastructural Facilities

The District has an excellent road and railway transport network. The District has 76 Electrical Sub-Stations with 16784 kms. of H.T. and 23003 kms. of L.T. lines. The District possess a network of Tanks, Wells and Canals for irrigation purpose. All the municipalities and principal town in the District are provided with protected water supply.

Banks Facilities

Syndicate Bank is the lead Bank of the District. There are 193 Commercial Bank Branches. One branch of A.P. State Finance Corporation, 13 branches of Co-operative Central Banks are operative in the district.

Industrial Potential in Anantapur District

Resource based Industries include the (a) Sericulture (Agro-based), (b) Mineral based, (c) Demand based Industries.

Table 3.6 : Bank-wise Deposits and Credits in Anantapur District as on March, (1990)

Sl. No.	*Name of the Bank*	*Number Branch*	*Deposit*	*Agri.*	*S.S.I.*	*Pri- Self Emp.*	*Trade*	*other*
1.	State Bank of India	32	99735	352415	94315	9872	19458	27846
2.	State Bank of Hyderabad	1	17646	—	1623	—	729	324
3.	State Bank of Mysore	1	15611	287	296	254	1369	·349
4.	Andhra Bank	22	487563	77544	52	—	11165	13790
5.	Canara Bank	10	163924	65066	6908	2175	55599	1991
6.	Corporation Bank	6	83789	23379	7510	1651	4345	1708
7.	Indian Bank	1	28420	2068	606	1498	663	491
8.	Syndicate Bank	30	486810	140721	24337	7985	27409	18366
9.	Union Bank of India	1	9262	4891	280	165	228	375
10.	Vijaya Bank	2	34618	8140	2530	2029	2371	518
11.	Karnataka Bank Ltd.	4	43264	5311	536	362	1145	690
12.	The Vysya Bank Ltd.	12	277813	30183	12357	1750	22653	6655
13.	Karur Vysya Bank Limited	1	10828	92	372	—	100	388
14.	Sri Ananta Grameena Bank	69	202820	201945	27597	—	31271	2423
15.	UCO Bank	1	5543	139	118	111	504	36
	Total	**193**	**2768646**	**912181**	**201137**	**27852**	**129009**	**76006**

(a) Sericulture

Mulberry cultivations are growing fast in the district 64,000 acres, producing 15000 Mts. of Cocoons yearly. At present, only 5000 Mts of Cocoons are being used by the local units. The remaining Cocoons production is exported to the adjoining Karnataka State. Hence, there is good scope for the establishment of Silk Reeling Units.

(b) Mineral

There is already sufficient growth in slab polishing industry in the District as about 200 units are so far established. Granite stone is also available abundantly in the District. Hence, Granite stone polishing industries have been identified for promotion during the last five years. Polished granted slabs and Tiles are having good foreign market.

(c) Demand Based

The District is having very good skilled workers in candidates with Diploma certificates in various disciplines. There are nearly 3000 candidates on the Register of local Employment Exchange with ITI qualifications. Further, Hindupur in Anantapur District has been identified under the Growth Centre Concept Scheme for intensive industrial, development during the 8th Five Year Plan.

Institutional Support and Facilities for Finance:

The following organisations are helping the growth of industries by way of providing necessary counsultancy services, technical guidance and marketing assistance.

1) The District Industries Centre and the Commissionerate of Industries.
2) Small Industries Service Institute, Hyderabad.
3) Small Industries Extention Training Institute, Hyderabad.
4) Andhra Pradesh Industrial Technical Consultancy Organisation, Hyderabad.
5) The Andhra Pradesh Small-Scale Industries Development Corporation, Hyderabad.

Industrial Profile of the Anantapur District Large and Medium-Scale Industries

There are 22 large and medium-scale industries in Anantapur District of which 9 are Textile based 4 are food and chemical based, 3 are electrical and electronics, 3 are Mechanical and 3 are plastic and Rubber based.

Table 3.7 : Category-wise Distribution of Large and Medium-Scale Industries in Anantapur District

Sl. No.	*Category of Industries*	*No. of Units*	*Investment (in lakhs)*	*Employment (No. of Persons)*	*Average investment per Unit (Rs. in lakhs)*	*Capital employment Ratio*
1.	Food and Agro Processing	6	900	470	150	1.92
2.	Textile	1	1000	900	1000	1.11
3.	Cement	4	11500	1700	2,875	6.76
4.	Electrical	5	3110	1710	622	1.82
5.	Mineral	1	93	340	93	3.66
6.	Engineering	17	7812	3252	459.5	2.40
7.	Others	1	800	30	800	26.67

Table 3.8 : Large and Medium-Scale Industries Existing

Sl. No.	*Name and Address of the Unit*	*Line of Manufacture*	*Capacity*	*Capital*	*Employment*
I. Mechanical					
1.	Pattabhi Limited Bukkarayasamudram	Un-machined Steel forgings	2000 TPA	145.96	48
2.	M/s. Shanti Casting Ltd. Industrial Development Area Thumukunta, Hindupur Mandal	Special Grade Casting	10000 TPA	73.10	40
3.	M/s. Karyo Bronze (P) Ltd. Plt No. 118 IDA Thumukunta, Hindupur	Precision non-ferms Casings (Handicrafts)	30 TPA	97.00	100
4.	M/s. M.G. Metallic Spring (P) Ltd., Bellary Road, Anantapur	Industrial Metallic Springs	350 TPA	63.55	61
5.	M/s. A.P. Power Tools Ltd., Balapathi (V) Hindupur Mandi	Electrical and Preumatic Industrial Power Tools	2.5 lakhs Nos. P.A.	321.31	74
II. Electrical & Electronics					
6.	M/s. A.P. Lightings Ltd., Assisted Pvt. Industrial Estate, Anantapur.	G.L.S. Lamps	12 Milli-ion	129.00	252
7.	M/s. Hyderabad Allwyn Ltd., Penukonda	Watch Assembly	3 lakhs Nos. P.A.	27.00	152
III. Food & Chemical Based					
8.	Nizam Sugar Factory Ltd., Near Parigi, Hindupur	Sugar	Sugarcane Crushing	472.00	500

(Contd.)

Table 3.8 : (Contd.)

Sl. No.	Name and Address of the Unit	Line of Manufacture	Capacity	Capital	Employment
9.	M/s. A.P. Oil Seed Vegetable Oil Complex, Taponagar, Anantapur	G.N. Oil & Solvent Extraction	25 TPD	110.00	90
10.	M/s. Polytech Organics Ltd., Anantapur	1. Liquid Glucose	3000 TPA	188.00	137
		2. Calcium Lactage	50 TPA		
		3. Organic Acid	500 TPA		
		4. Calcium Gluconate	100 TPA		
11.	M/s. Suman Metalogical Chemical Product Ltd., Shed. No. 729–D Gooty Road, Guntakal	Copper Power Sodium Thifd sulphate Re-oxide piments	600 TPA 1500 TPA 800 TPA	224.00	130
12.	M/s. Madhu Solvent Extractions (P) Ltd., Goody	Solvent Extraction oil Deoiled Cake	2100 TPA 27099 TPA	137.00	100
IV.	**<u>Plastic : Rubber Based</u>**				
13.	M/s. Elgi Tyres Trades Ltd., Kirikera, Hindupur	1. Precured Tyre Threads	450 TPA	276.00	196
14.	M/s. Monarch Pipes (P) Ltd., Hampapuram, Anantapur	P.V.C. Rigid Pipes	500 TPA	230.00	91
15.	M/s. Dada Brothers Ltd., Dada Hills, Penukonda	Reclaimed Rubber	3000 TPA	250.00	116
16.	M/s. Dhananjya Plastics, 51, I.D.A., Thumukunta, Hindupur	Printed Multilayer Co-extended Plastic film	1750 TPA	548.00	32

(Contd.)

Table 3.8 : (Contd.)

Sl. No.	Name and Address of the Unit	Line of Manufacture	Capacity	Capital	Employment
V. Mineral Based					
17.	M/s. Bharath Gold Mines, Ramagiri	Gold	697.5 Grams PD	570.00	416
18.	M/s. Prime Granites (P) Ltd., I.D.A. Thumukunta, Hindupur	Cut and Polished Granite Monuments	10000 Sq. Mts.	140.00	16
VI. Textile Industries					
19.	M/s. Super Spinning Mills Ltd., Kirikera Hindupur	Cotton Yarn	50548 Spindles	1208.00	1080
20.	M/s. Premier Cotton Spinning Mills, Kodigenehalli, Hindupur.	Cotton Yarn	49920 Spindles	2142.00	1154
21.	M/s. The Andhra Co-op. Spinning Mills Ltd., Gooty Road, Guntakal.	Cotton Yarn	50000 Spindles	231.00	1809
22.	M/s. The Anantapur Cotton Mills, N.T.C. (APKH & M) Ltd., Yerraguntapalli, Tadapartiri	Cotton Yarn	32188 Spindles	181.55	447
23.	M/s. Super Spinning Mills Unit, Kotnur, Hindupur	Cotton Yarn	49920 Spindles	1971.00	1148
24.	M/s. Anantapur Mulberry Silks Ltd., Somanadoddi, Anantapur	Bleaching Dyeing and Printing of Cotton Silk and Polyster	12000 Mts.	147.00	70

(Contd.)

Table 3.8 : (Contd.)

Sl. No.	*Name and Address of the Unit*	*Line of Manufacture*	*Capacity*	*Capital*	*Employment*
25.	M/s. R.P.G. Tyram Processing Unit, Hindupur.	Yarn Processing	1500 TPA	121.00	182
26.	M/s. Maruthi Gold Starsilks Ltd., Penukonda	Raw Silkyarn	2400 Ends 500 TPA	744.00	737
27.	M/s. Richman Silks Limited, Chilamathur	Export Oriented Silk Cloth	5 lakhs meters	1300.00	206
28.	M/s. Supreme Textile Processing Ltd., Moda (V) Hindupur	Polyster Yarn Cotton Yarn Processing	1000 Kgs. PD	6.00	29
				12113.47	**9413**

Table 3.9 : Small-Scale Industries Established as on 31-03-1992

Sl. No.	*Category*	*No. of units*	*Invest- ment Rs. in lakhs*	*Emp- loy- ment*	*Type of Industries*
1.	Agro	1528	971.68	8478	Oil Mills, Rice Mills Flour Mills, Food Products, Tamarind Starch, Coffee Powder etc.,
2.	Engineering	1077	785.67	5280	Engineering Workshops Automobile, Servicing Steel Furniture, Tincans Builders hard works, Allumnium Cables, DPC Wires ACSR Conductors, Alloy Casting, Foundrys Bus body builders etc.,
3.	Forest	358	123.44	2047	Saw Mills, Wooden Furniture, Gisalfibre extraction, Ropes manufacturing etc.,
4.	Textile	654	437.07	5879	Silk Reeling and Twist ing and Readymade Garment Powerlooms, Hosiery etc.
5.	Livestock	76	19.12	316	Tanning, Leather Goods, Bone Meal etc.
6.	Mineral	597	886.68	5278	Slab Polishing, Mineral Pulversing, Mosaic, Chips Readmetal etc.,
7.	Chemical	177	367.09	1390	Match, Soap Cleaning powder Phynoil, PVC Pipes, Polythene Bags, Burnt Line etc.
8.	Miscellaneous	561	389.00	2367	Printing, X-ray Units, Exercise Note Books Pencils Rigset.
	Total	**5028**	**3976.75**	**31035**	

Small-Scale Industries

There are 5022 Small Industries in the District with an investment of Rs. 3976.75 crores providing employment to 31,035 persons.

Category-wise distribution of Small-Scale Industrial Units in Anantapur District.

Table 3.10

Sr. No.	*Category*	*No. of units*	*Fixed Capital investment (Rs. in lakhs)*	*Employment*
1.	Agro based	1528	971.68	8478
2.	Engineering	1077	785.67	5280
3.	Forest based	358	123.44	2047
4.	Textile	654	437.07	5879
5.	Livestock	76	19.12	316
6.	Mineral	597	886.68	5278
7.	Chemical	177	367.09	1390
8.	Miscellaneous	561	389.00	2367
	Total	**5022**	**3976.75**	**31035**

Table 3.11 : Small-Scale Industries in Anantapur District

Year	*Units*	*Employment*	*Total Investment Rs. in lakhs*
1978–79	35	181	67.18
1979–80	132	914	81.14
1980–81	160	2063	107.09
1981–82	194	1431	139.16
1982–83	220	1349	136.63
1983–84	269	2081	226.16
1984–85	282	1300	152.60
1985–86	301	1592	387.13
1986–87	328	2002	410.97
1987–88	390	2109	417.51
1988–89	432	2602	727.54
1989–90	423	2009	415.98
1990–91	502	2441	502.51

Total 28 Medium and Large-Scale Industries in Anantapur District.
Source : Anantapur District Industries Centre, Anantapur.

Table 3.12 A : Industrial Co-operatives

a)	No. of Industrial Co-operative Societies Registered	121
b)	No. of Working Societies	47
c)	No. of Dormant Societies	58
d)	No. of Societies taken up for liquidation	16

Central Subsidy/State Incentives

S. No.	*Scheme*	*No. of Units benefited*	*Amount (Rs. in lakhs)*
1.	Central Investment subsidy	760	489.54
2.	State Investment Subsidy	111	129.56
3.	State Investment Subsidy for SC's	201	8.98
4.	Interest free sales-tax loan	10	21.34
5.	Difference of Sales tax	77	305.54
6.	Power subsidy for 4th and 5th year	7	10.01
7.	Certificates issued for 25% power rebate for first three years	146	—

Table 3.12 B

S. No.	*Social Status Wise*	*Total No. of Beneficiaries*	*Sl. No.*	*Trade-wise*	*No.*
1.	S.C.	315	1.	Silk Wearing	21
2.	S.T.	136	2.	Cumbly Weaving	4
3.	Backward Communities	908	3.	Slab Polishing	4
4.	Others	18	4.	Handloom Weaving action	2
			5.	Lime Burning	2
			6.	Bamboo & Basket making	3
			7.	Tanning	1
			8.	Leather Puppets	1
			9.	Pottery	1
			10.	Multi Traders	8
	Total	**1377**			**47**

Table 3.13 : Artisan Complexes Established

Silk Weaving				
1. Gorantla	Gorantla	BC	20	20,000
2. Muddireddipalli	Hindupur	BC	51	12,000
3. Gandlavandla Palli	Mudigubba	BC	35	9,000
4. Thirmaladev	Nallacheruvu	BC	16	11,120
5. Sivapalli	Dharmavaram	BC	20	11,120
6. Somandepalli	Somandepalli	BC	40	3,600
7. Kristipadu	Peddavaduguru	BC	20	11,120
8. Yadiki	Yadiki	BC	57	11,120
9. Gannevaripalli	Tadipatri	BC	118	11,120
10. Peddireddipalli	Parigi	BC	22	11,120
11. Kesepalli	Singanamala	BC	15	11,120
12. Nyamaddala	C.K. Palli	BC	28	11,120
13. Cholasamudram	Lepakshi	BC	53	12,000
14. Vadiampeta	Garladinne	BC	16	11,120
15. Guttur	Penukonda	BC	22	12,000
16. Somandepalli-2	Somandepalli	BC	41	30,000
17. Peddavauduguru	Peddavaduguru	BC	20	12,000
18. Yadiki	Yadiki	BC	48	30,000
19. Peddapappur	Peddapappur	BC	45	30,000
20. Lepakshi	Lepakshi	BC	16	30,000
21. Somandepalli	Somandepalli	BC	15	30,000
Cumbly Weaving				
22. P. Siddarampuram	Atmakur	BC	20	7,800
23. Atmakur	Atmakur	BC	20	7,800
24. Kurlapalli	Kalyandur	BC	17	7,800
25. B. Byadegera	Agali	BC	16	7,800
Slab Polishing				
26. China	Tadipatri	SC	25	24,000
27. Gooty	Gooty	SC	30	25,000
28. Bhogasamudram	Tadipatri	SC	30	25,000
29. Hussainapuram	Tadipatri	SC	190	50,000

Contd.

Table 3.13 : (Contd.)

Handloom				
30. Konapuram	Hindupur	SC	10	10,000
31. Chinnapolamada	Tadipatri	BC	14	12,000
Bamboo & Basket				
32. Devarintipalli	Nallamada	SC	20	10,000
33. Reddivaripalli	Tanakal	ST	25	7,800
34. Ananthasagaram	Bathalapalli	ST	16	7,200
Lime Burning				
35. Nimmalakunta	Dharmavaram	ST	10	1,650
36. Makkajipalli	Penukonda	ST	18	8,500
Tanning				
37. Chigicherla	Dharmavaram	ST	20	5,000
Leather Puppet Mfg.				
38. Nimmalakunta	Dharmavaram	BC	10	5,000
Pottery				
39. Vajrakarur	Vajrakarur	BC	16	4,000
Multi-Functional				
40. Gangavaram	Beluguppa	Others	6	6,300
		SC	2	
		BC	8	
41. Kambadur	Kambadur	Others	4	6,200
		SC	9	
		BC	9	
42. Amarapuram	Amarapuram	Others	2	9,200
		BC	18	
43. Kothacheruvu	Kothacheruvu	Others	2	8,400
44. D. Hirehal	D. Hirehal	Others	1	7,200
		SC	5	
		ST	11	
45. Uddehal	Bommanhal	Others		8,200
		SC	10	
		ST	6	

(Contd.)

Table 3.13 : (Contd.)

46. Chinnamustoor	Uravakonda	Others	3	5,758
		SC	8	
		BC	2	
47. Yellanur	Yellanur	SC	7	7,600
		ST	4	
		BC	3	

Table 3.14 : Comparison of Anantapur District with State (A.P.) Particulars of Urban Population in India, A.P. Anantapur in 1981

(Rs. in lakhs)

Urban 1991	*Anantapur*	*A.P. State*	*% of State*
	5.31	*124.88*	*4.25*
Density of Population			
1991	133	195	68.02
Literates (No. Lakhs)	29.02	159.26	4.64
b) Literacy %	7.39	29.94	—
Working Population	1087	226.06	4.81
SC	3.49	79.62	4.38
ST	0.82	31.76	2.58
BC	8.28	–	–
Colleges & Other Educational Institutions	14.00	–	–
Junior Colleges attached with High Schools	17.00	–	–
Junior Colleges (Independent)	11.00	–	–
Engg. Colleges	1.00	–	–
polytechnic Colleges	2.00	–	–
I.T.I.	6.00		
High Schools	230.00		
Hospitals 2 Dispensaries	87.00		
Vilage Electrified %	941.00 (100 %)		
No. of Universities	2.00	8	25 %

Table 3.15

Year	*Units*	*Employment*	*Total Investment Rs. in lakhs*
1978–79	35	181	67.18
1979–80	132	914	81.14
1980–81	160	2063	107.09
1981–82	194	1431	139.16
1982–83	220	1349	136.63
1983–84	269	2081	226.16
1984–85	282	1300	152.60
1985–86	301	1592	387.13
1986–87	328	2002	410.97
1987–88	390	2109	417.51
1988–89	432	2602	727.54
1989–90	423	2009	415.98
1990–91	502	2441	502.51

Source : District Industries Centre, Anantapur.

Table 3.16 : Achievements of District Industries in Anantapur District

Sl. No.	*Category*		*S.S.I.*	*Employment*	*Rs. in lakhs fixed Investment*	*Yearly Production value Rs. in lakhs*
1.	Agro :	1990–91	98	402	91.60	363.50
		1991–92	98	462	119.20	344.50
2.	Forest :	1990–91	25	830	37.00	65.00
		1991–92	32	865	41.50	74.00
3.	Textile :	1990–91	75	1395	108.00	214.00
		1991–92	95	1520	112.00	229.00
4.	Engineering & Allied	1990–91	83	530	27.50	58.50
		1991–92	63	608	101.00	233.00
5.	Chemical Base	1990–91	16	114	40.00	96.00
		1991–92	18	128	56.00	153.00
6.	Other Industries	1990–91	11	447	29.60	38.00
		1991–92	6	422	13.80	25.00

Source : Asstt. Director of Mines & Geologes, Anantapur.

Table 3.17 : Mineral Revenue Collected the Year 1989–90

Sl. No.	*Name of the Mineral*	*Production in Mts.*	*Despatches in Mts.*	*Total Mineral Revenue Collected*
I.	**Major Minerals** :			
1.	Iron ore	a) Lumps	–	–
		b) Fixes	138685	134900
2.	Lime stone		30875	30320
3.	Steatite		2192	2160
4.	White Clay & Natural Clay		4520	4290
5.	White shale		5900	5875
6.	Serpentire		56480	55259
7.	Dolamite		462	400
8.	Calcite		1284	1250
9.	Barytes		–	–
10.	Green Quartz		–	–
11.	Corrudum (Kgs.)		56.540	–
12.	Gold ore		–	–
13.	Soap stone		–	–
14.	Phyro Phillite		1040	1000
II.	**Minor Minerals** :			
1.	Multicolour Granite		768	638 cbm
2.	Black Granite		93.712 cbm	105 dbm
3.	Grey Granite		1002 cbm	937 cbm
4.	Rechmath Granite		–	200 mts.
5.	Napa slabs		28130 sq. mts.	97125 sq. mts.
6.	Road metal and Building stone		2990 cbm	

Source : Hand book of Statistics Anantapur District

Conclusion

After establishment of District Industries centres, Small-Scale Industrialisation has taken at a rapid place in respect of large-scale, small-scale and rural industries, Resource endowments particularly agricultural, and mineral suggest that there is ample potentially for locating agro based and mineral based industries, in the district. A well conceived programme of developing infrastructural facilities and expanding the promotional institution and extending the central and state incentives to backward blocks, is required to remove the inbalances and pave the way for balanced industries development in the district.

References

1. Desai Vasant, Problems and prospects of Small-Scale Industries New Delhi, Deep Publications 1984 pp. 110-112.
2. Government of India (DCSSI), A Hand Book of Extension Services for Rural Industrial Develoment, New Delhi. Development Commissioner, Small-Scale Industries, Ministry of Industry, 1980, pp. 85-86.
3. Task force consists of General Manager, DIC (Chairman Deputy Director, Credit (Convernor), District Employment Officer (Member) Lead Bank Officer (Member), State Bank of India Official (Member) and Local Bank representative (Member) including National Institution of Small industries Extention Training, Small Industries service Institue and productivity Council.
4. Government of Andhra Pradesh G.O. Ms. No. 761 - Annexure 111, Dt. 3.10.1978.
5. Op. Cit. "A Hand Book" p. 7,
6. G.O. Ms. No. 761, Annexure 111, dated 03.19.1978.

4

Capital Structure of Selected Units

Introduction

Industrialization helps the process of capital formation and enables the country to build up the stock of capital asset formation, mobilisation of savings and their investment in capital assets is thus a vital prerequisite of economic development. Increases in capital formation generally follow the increases in added value, generated in the process of economic development. The growth of the industrial sector creates a strong base for the transformation of savings in the productive capital and the ready augmentation of the stocks of productive assets.

Historically, savings generated in the agricultural sector have played a valuable role in financing industrialisation in many countries like Japan and Taiwan. Even in the present day underdeveloped countries savings generated in the agricultural sector could be utilised for sustaining industrial development.

The main objectives of the programmes for the development of the small industries have been to create large-scale employment opportunities to promote decentralization and dispersal of industries to develop agro based and ancillary industries to improve the skills of artisans and quality of their products, reduce the role of subsides and step up the production of consumer goods and other essential articles and those that are having large potential for exports.

Nature of Activity of Sample Units

Sample units classified into seven categories, have been selected for the study at random in Anantapur District.

It can be observed from the Table 4.1 that the sample chosen, Engineering occupied the first position with 124 (25.3 per cent) units, followed by Agro-based with 120 (24.2 per cent) units, miscellaneous 115 (23.2 per cent) units, textile with 35 (8.4 per cent) units, Chemical 24 (7.4 per cent) Units. Forests 29 (7.4 per cent) units and Mineral 20 (4.2 per cent) units.

Table 4.1 : Category-wise Distribution of Units

Sl. No.	*Category*	*Total Number in the Study Areas*	*Number of Sample Units*	*20%*
1.	Agro based	120	23	(24.2)
2.	Engineering	124	24	(25.3)
3.	Forest-based	29	7	(7.4)
4.	Textile based	35	8	(8.4)
5.	Mineral based	20	4	(4.2)
6.	Chemical	34	7	(7.4)
7.	Miscellaneous	115	22	(23.2)
	All	**477 Total**	**95**	**100.00**

Note : Figures in Parentheses indicate percentage to total.
Source : Field Survey

In order to find out, inter industry disparities in distribution of sample units standard deviation (S.D) and Co-efficient of variation (C.V.) are computed. The higher degree of dispersion of units between categories of industries (S.D. = 8.26 and C.V. 61%) is deserved from the results.

Occupational Background and Location

Of the main occupations, Agro based and forest based industries are controlled by families which are directly involved in agriculture. Most of the units are inherited by the families. In the case of other units, others irrespective of their family occupation are interested in starting the units.

However, different factors influence the entrepreneurs to choose particular unit and an attempt is made in the following lines to examine what made the Small-Scale Industries to select the activity in which they are engaged in and how they feel about the suitability of their industrial location.

Data pertaining to occupational back ground and locational suitability of the sample units are presented in Table 4.2

Table 4.2 : Occupational Background and Location of Sample Units

Sl. No.	*Category*	*Occupational Background Location*				
		Started by the present generation	Heriditary	Suitable	Non-Suitable	Total Units
1.	Agro based	19	4	15	8	23
2.	Engineering	13	11	18	6	24
3.	Forest-based	5	2	5	2	7
4.	Textile based	5	3	6	2	8
5.	Mineral based	2	2	3	1	4
6.	Chemical	2	5	6	1	7
7.	Miscellaneous	13	9	15	7	22
	Total	**59** (62)	**36** (38)	**68** (72)	**27** (28)	**95** 9100)

Note : Figures in Parentheses indicate percentage to total
Source : Field Survey

Out of total 95 sample units, 59 (62 per cent) units started by the present generation and 36 (38 per cent) units are inherited. 19 units in Agro, 130 units in Engineering out of 24 units, 5 units out of 8 in Textile, 2 units out of 4 units in Mineral, 2 Units out of 7 units in Chemical and 13 units out of 22 units in Miscellaneous have been started by the present generation. 72 per cent of the respondents expressed that the location of area is suitable to carry on their industrial activity, whereas the rest of the respondents felt that the location was not suitable, as per the Table 4.2.

Social Status of Sample Units

Regarding Social Status, it is observed from the below table that out of 95 units 3 (6.32 per cent) belong to S.C. communities, 7 (7.37) to Backward Castes. 82 units to forward caste, (86.32 per cent).

Schedule Caste respondents are found family in Agro, Forest and Textile based industries (33 per cent) respectively. Scheduled tribes respondents are not found in any category, whereas backward communities are mostly in all categories, except Engineering and Chemical industries. Forward Caste respondents 82 units (86.3 per cent). This shows that majority of the Schedule Caste, Schedule Tribe and backward community respondents are found in their community - oriented traditional occupations due to lack of occupational mobility.

Table 4.3 : Social Status of Sample Units

S.No.	*Category*	S.C.	S.T.	B.C.	F.C.	Total Units
1.	Agro based	2	–	1	20	23
2.	Engineering	–	–	–	24	24
3.	Forest-based	2	–	1	4	7
4.	Textile based	2	–	1	5	8
5.	Mineral based	–	–	1	3	4
6.	Chemical	–	–	–	7	7
7.	Miscellaneous	–	–	3	19	22
	Total	6 (6.32)		7 (7.37)	82 (86.32)	95 (100)

S.C. = Scheduled Caste S.T. = Scheduled Tribe
B.C. = Backward Caste F.C. = Forward Caste

Note : Figures in Parentheses indicate percentage to total

Source : Field Survey

Educational Status of Sample Units

Educational Status of Sample Small-Scale Industries units are presented in Table 4.4

It is noticed form the above table that 23 respondents (24.3 per cent) are illiterates who can not read and write any language,

Table 4.4 : Educational Status of Sample Units

Sl. No.	*Category*	*Level of Education of Respondents*			Total
		Illiterate	School Level	College Level	
1.	Agro based	7	14	2	23
2.	Engineering	5	15	4	24
3.	Forest	2	4	1	7
4.	Textile	2	3	3	8
5.	Mineral	–	–	4	4
6.	Chemical	–	3	4	7
7.	Miscellaneous	7	10	5	22
	Total	**23 (24.3)**	**49 (51.58)**	**23 (24.3)**	**95 (100)**

Note : Figures in parentheses indicate percentage to total
Source : Field Survey

49 respondents (51.58 per cent) are of school level who can read and write Telugu language as they have formal schooling, 23 (24.3. per cent) respondents have vollgiate education. In Mineral and Chemical all the respondents are of collegiate education.

Source of Inputs and Markets

Small-Scale Industries Units are largely based on locally available raw materials to meet the needs of local people. Data relating to the sources of inputs and markets are presented in Table 4.5.

58 sample units (61.1 per cent) are procuring raw materials locally. 18 out of 24 units in Engineering, 6 out of 7 units in Forest based industries, 4 out of 8 units in Textile, Mineral 3 out of 4 units, and 14 out of 22 units in Miscellaneous industries are getting raw materials from out side the district.

It is noticed that regarding markets for the sample units 43 (45.3 per cent) of the units have market for their produce within the District, where as 52, (54.7 per cent) have both with in and out side the district. The number of units having local market is less than the number of units having local as well as outside the district.

Table 4.5 : Social Status of Sample Units

S. No.	*Category*	Source of in-puts within the Distt.	Out-side the Distt.	Within Distt.	Both outside inside the Distt.	Total
1.	Agro based	13	10	15	8	23
2.	Engineering	18	6	13	21	24
3.	Forest-based	6	1	3	4	7
4.	Textile based	4	4	3	5	8
5.	Mineral based	3	1	1	3	4
6.	Chemical	–	7	1	6	7
7.	Miscellaneous	14	8	7	15	22
	Total	**58 (61.1)**	**37 (38.9)**	**43 (45.3)**	**52 (54.7)**	**95 (100)**

Note : Figures in parentheses indicate percentage to total
Source : Field Survey

Capital structural of Small-Scale Industrial Units Working Capital

The Table 4.6 shows the working capital of the sample units. 26 per cent (25 units) working capital which is less than Rs. 5000, 13 per cent (12 units) posses the working capital in the range of Rs. 5,000 - Rs. 10,000, 16 per cent (15 units) operate with working capital in the range of Rs., 30,000 - Rs. 60,000 19 per cent (18 units) operate with working capital Rs. 60,000 - Rs. 1,00,000 and above, 25 (26 per cent) units ranging from Rs. 10,000-Rs. 30,000, 16 units are in the range of less than Rs. 5,000 in Engineering industrial units. 13 units ranging from Rs. 5,000 - Rs. 10,000, in this range Miscellaneous industries are more that is 8 units out of 13 units.

Fixed Capital

Fixed capital is a pre-requisite to start an industrial unit. For establishment of Small-Scale Industrial units, the major sources of fixed capital are Banks and State Finance Corporation (S.F.C.). The District Industries Centre recommends to S.F.C. and Banks for providing the fixed capital loan to small-scale industrial units.

Fixed Capital of the sample units is presented in the Table 4.7.

Table 4.6 : Distribution of Sample Units by the Size of Working Capital

Sl. No.	Category	No. of Units	Rs. less less than Rs.5,000	Rs.5000–10,000	Rs.10,000–30,000	Rs.30,000–60,000	Rs.60,000–1,00,000	Above 1,00,000	Average value of working capital
1.	Agro	23	1	2	8	6	3	4	28,000
2.	Engineering	24	16	2	6	–	–	–	6,947
3.	Forest	7	3	1	–	3	–	–	16,000
4.	Textile	8	1	–	3	2	2	–	29,600
5.	Mineral	4	–	–	1	–	–	3	83,333
6.	Chemical	7	–	–	1	1	2	3	1,19,400
7.	Miscellaneous	22	4	8	6	3	–	1	16,353
	Total	**95**	**25** (26)	**12** (13)	**25** (26)	**15** (16)	**7** (7)	**11** (12)	**3,00,433**
	S.D.								38849
	C.V.								91 %

Note : Figures in parentheses are percentages to total.

Source : Field Survey.

Table 4.7 : Distribution of Sample Units by the Size of Fixed Capital

Sl. No.	*Category*	*5000–10000*	*10000 –30000*	*30000 –60000*	*60000 –100000*	*Above 100000*	*Average value of working capital*
1.	Agro	1 (4.33)	5 (21.7)	3 (13.04)	9 (39.13)	5 (121.7)	91,555
2.	Engineering	–	10 (41.6)	7 (29.17)	4 (16.67)	3 (12.5)	40,000
3.	Forest	–	–	3 (42.86)	2 (28.57)	2 (28.57)	66,000
4.	Textile	–	2 (25.00)	2 (25.00)	2 (25.00)	2 (25.00)	75,400
5.	Mineral	–	–	–	2 (50.00)	2 (50.00)	1,26,666
6.	Chemical	–	–	–	2 (28.57)	2 (71.43)	1,74,000
7.	Miscella-neous	2 (9.09)	2 (9.09)	4+2 (27.27)	3 (13.64)	9 (40.91)	81,818
Total (95) (100.00)		**3 (32.00)**	**19 (20.00)**	**21 (22.00)**	**24 (25.00)**	**28 (30.00)**	**6,55,439**
	S.D.						40,825
	C.V.						44 %

Note : Figures in parentheses are percentages to total.

Source : Field Survey.

The average value of fixed capital is higher than working capital in all units and there is no exception as these being small-scale industries. About 39.13% units in Agro based industries required Fixed Capital ranging from Rs.. 60,000 to 1,00,000/- about 21.7 per cent units required Fixed Capital ranging from above Rs. 1,00,000. The units having Fixed Capital less than Rs. 60,000/- at about 13.04 per cent. Units below Rs. 30,000/- at about 26 per cent. Engineering units abut 41.67 per cent and 29.17 per cent required fixed capital ranging from Rs. 10,000/- to Rs. 30,000/- and Rs. 30,000/- to Rs. 60,000/- respectively. There are no Textile, Forest and Chemical units which required Fixed Capital less than Rs. 10,000/-. All industries in Forest sector range between Rs. 30,000/- to Rs. 1,00,000/-

. In the same way all Mineral industries required fixed Capital of Rs. 60,000/- and above only. The Chemical industries required Fixed Capital of Rs. 60,000/- to Rs. 1,00,000/- at about 28.57 per cent and Rs. 1,00,000 above 71.43 per cent units, th miscellaneous 40.91 per cent tunis required fixed capital above Rs. 1,00,000. 27.27 per cent units required fixed capital from Rs. 30,000/- to Rs. 60,000/-.

Composition of the Total Capital of Sample Units is given in the Table 4.8. On the whole, the ratio of fixed capital to working capital is 69:31. The ratio of fixed capital to working capital of these seven industries is 77:23, 85:15, 80:20, 72:28, 60:40, 59:41, 83:17. In all the categories, fixed Capital is higher than that of working capital. In Agro-based industries fixed capital (77 per cent) working capital (23 per cent). In engineering based industries Fixed Capital is (85 per cent) and working capital (15 per cent). In Forest based industries, Fixed Capital is (80 per cent) and working capital

Table 4.8 : Composition of Capital in Sample Units

Sl. No.	*Category*	No. of Samples Units	Average working Capital	Average fixed Capital	Average Total Capital
1.	Agro based	120 (23)	28,000 (23)	91,555 (77)	1,19,555
2.	Engineering	124 (24)	6,947 (15)	40,000 (85)	46,947
3.	Forest-based	29 (7)	16,800 (20)	66,000 (80)	82,800
4.	Textile based	35 (8)	29,600 (28)	75,400 (72)	1,05,000
5.	Mineral based	20 (4)	83,333 (40)	1,26,666 (50)	2,09,999
6.	Chemical	34 (7)	1,19,400 (41)	1,74,000 (59)	2,93,400
7.	Miscellaneous	115 (22)	16,353 (17)	81,818 (83)	98,171
	S.D.	477 (95)	3,00,433	6,55,439	9,55,872
	C.V.		(31)	(69)	(100)

Note : Figures in parentheses indicate percentage to total

Source : Field Survey

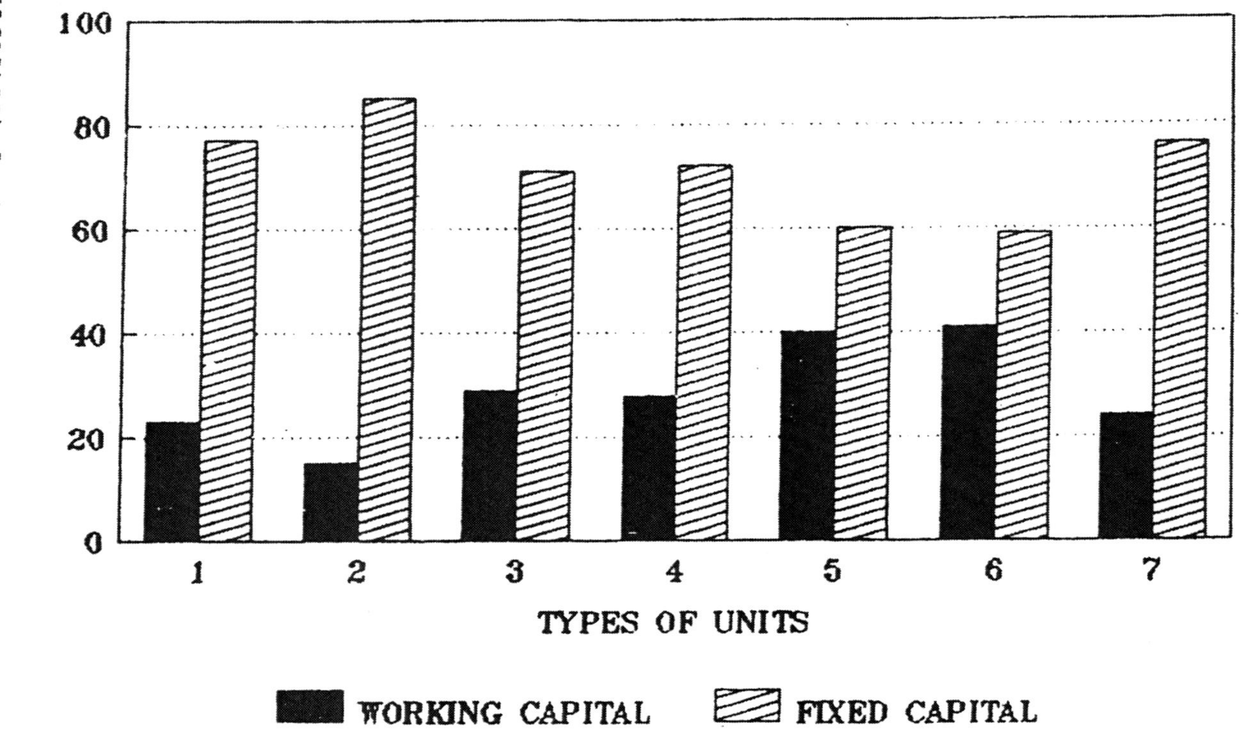

Composition of Capital in Sample Units

20 per cent). In Textile based industries Fixed Capital is (72 per cent) and working capital (28 percent) Mineral based industries Fixed Capital is (60 per cent), working capital is (40 per cent). In Chemical based industries fixed capital is (59 per cent) working capital (41 per cent). In Miscellaneous, fixed capital (83 per cent), working capital (17 per cent).

Sources of Finance of Sample Units (Industry Wise)

It may be noted that 35.2 per cent of investment is from their own funds, 29.3 per cent of investment by Banks, 29.8 per cent of financial assistance by State Finance Corporation (S.F.C) the remaining 5.7 per cent from other sources.

Among the 7 industrial categories, own finance is the highest in Textile (47.9) followed by Miscellaneous (47.4 per cent) and in Forest Industries (41.1 per cent), Mineral (34.5 per cent), Agro (19.6 per cent), Chemical (11.3 per cent) and in Engineering works industries (4.3 per cent) Bank Finance constitutes the highest proportion of Fixed Capital in Chemical (40.1 per cent) Agro (39.5 per cent) in other industries it ranges between 12.0 and 34.6 per cent. S.F.C. Finance are the highest in Chemical industries (45.6. per cent) and in other categories they ranged between 14.9 to 34.9 per cent.

Table 4.9 : Source of Finance

Sl. No.	*Source*	*Amount*	*Percent*
1.	Own Funds	36,40,148	35.2
2.	Banks	30,35,476	29.3
3.	State Finance Corporation	30,82,264	29.8
4.	Other Sources	5,91,763	5.7
	Total	**1,03,49,651**	**100.00**

In Table the contribution of different sources to the total capital investment of all different categories of sample units is presented. Proportion of own funds is higher in the case of Miscellaneous (48 per cent) followed by Textile (47 per cent). Assistance from Bank constituted an important source of finance in the case of Engineering (35 per cent), Textile (33 per cent), Agro (32 per cent), Chemical (30 per cent) and borrowing from State Finance Corporation is high in Chemical (36 per cent) followed by Agro

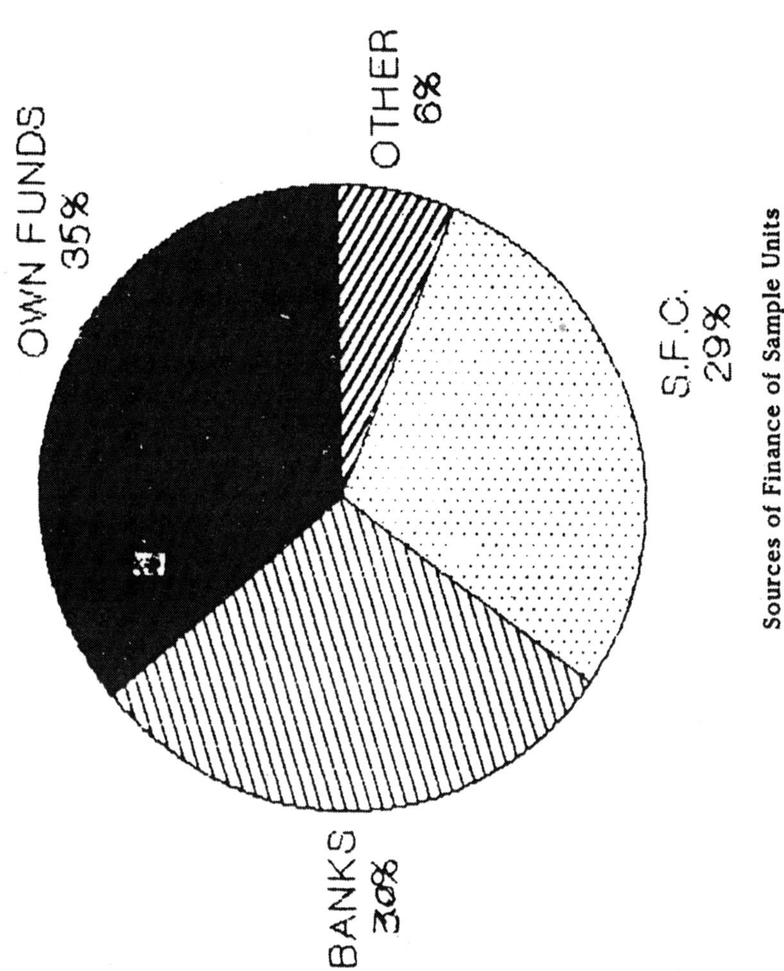

Sources of Finance of Sample Units

Table 4.10

Sl. No.	Category of Industries	Own	Bank	S.F.C.	Other Sources	Total	Total
1.	Agro	7,69,934 (28)	8,79.925 (32)	9,34,920 (34)	1,64,986 (6)	100	27,49,765
2.	Engineering	2,70,415 (24)	3,94,355 (35)	3,26,751 (29)	1,35,207 (12)	100	11,26,728
3.	Forest	2,37,636 (41)	1,27,512 (22)	1,68,084 (29)	46,368 98)	100	5,79,600
4.	Textile	3,94,800 (47)	2,77,200 (33)	1,68,000 (20)	—	100	8,40,000
5.	Mineral	2,93,999 (35)	2,43,599 (29)	2,26,798 (27)	75,600 (9)	100	8,39,996
6.	chemical	6,36,678 (31)	6,16,140 (30)	7,39,368 (36)	61,614 (3)	100	20,53,800
7.	Miscellaneous	10,36,686 (48)	4,96,745 (23)	5,18,343 (24)	1,07,988 (5)	100	21,59,762
	Total	**36,40,148**	**30,35,476**	**30,82,264**	**5,91,763**		**1,03,49,651**

based industries (34 per cent) Engineering and Forest (29 per cent), Mineral (27 per cent), Miscellaneous (24 per cent) and Textile (20 per cent). Other sources are high in Engineering (12 per cent) followed by Mineral (9 per cent). Source of finance of sample units industry wise is shown in figure.

Income and Capital Intensity

The value of Capital invested reflects the extent of out put produced and amount of income generated. Data is this regard are presented in Table 4.11.

Table 4.11 : Industrial Income and Capital Intensity

Sl. No.	*Category*	Output	Fixed Total Capital per Industry	Total Capital	Total Capital to out-put	Fixed Capital to out-put
1.	Agro based	26,73,382	1,19,555	27,49,765	1.03	22.36
2.	Engineering	24,29,640	46,947	11,26,728	2.16	51.75
3.	Forest-based	16,39,470	82,800	5,79,600	2.83	19.8
4.	Textile based	9,78,432	1,05,000	8,40,000	1.17	9.37
5.	Mineral based	29,44,480	2,09,099	8,39,996	3.52	8.36
6.	Chemical	21,63,861	2,93,400	20,53,800	1.05	20.56
7.	Miscellaneous	29,96,620	98,171	21,59,762	1.39	30.5
	Total	**1,58,26,245**	**9,55,872**	**1,03,49,651**	**13.15**	**162.24**

Source : Field Survey

Fixed capital per Industry of sample units stands at Rs. 10,421 and it is high in Chemical (Rs. 2,93,400) followed Mineral (Rs. 2,09,099) and the lowest fixed capital per industry is noticed in (Rs. 46,947), Engineering followed by forests (Rs. 82,800), Textile (Rs.1,05,000) and Agro (Rs. 1,19,555). Total output per industry of sample units stand at 1,79,000 and it is high in Mineral (Rs. 3,52,210) followed by Engineering (Rs.2,16,103) and the lowest total output Agro based industries (Rs. 1,03,322) followed by Chemical Rs. 1,05,431).

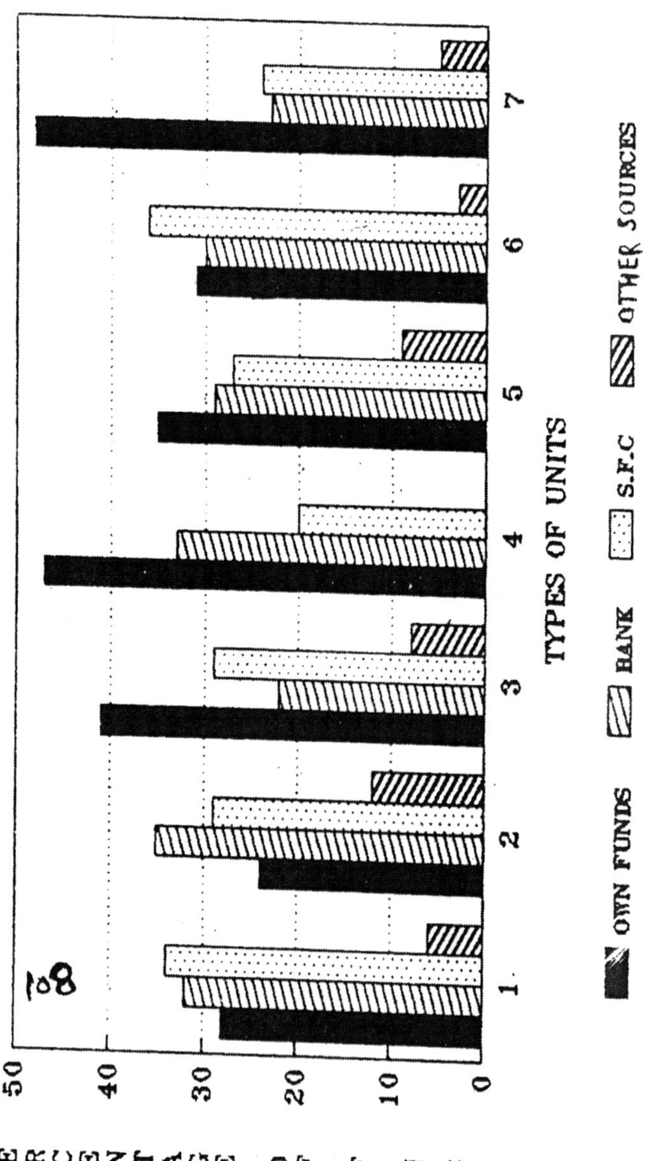

S.F.C : State Finance Corporation

Sources of Finance of Sample Units (Industry-wise)

Capital intensity as measured by the ratio of fixed capital to output is 15.59 and that of total capital to output is 1.52. Intensity is comparatively lesser in 7 categories of industries as indicated by capital output ratios. From the above analysis it can be inferred that labour intensity of small-scale industries is higher as they are more labour intensive and less capital intensive.

Output and Capital

The distribution of output and capital among different categories of units in the district is shown in Table 4.12, output of industrial units is influenced by the size in terms of capital, availability of the raw material and demand for the material produced, changing needs the people to suit present needs workers employed by the units.

Table 4.12

Sl. No.	*Category*	Output Yearly	Fixed Total Capital	Total Capital	Total Output Per Industry
1.	Agro based	24.08	1,19,555.00	27,49,765.00	1,04,696.00
2.	Engineering	48,24,840.00	46,947.00	11,26,728.00	2,01,035.00
3.	Forest-based	1,400.00	1,48,000.00	10,41,600.00	2,00,000.00
4.	Textile based	8,00,184.00	1,05,000.00	8,48,000.00	1,00,023.00
5.	Mineral based	26,99,700.00	2,09,099.00	8,36,396.00	6,74,925.00
6.	Chemical	67,176.00	2,93,400.00	20,53,000.00	4,70,232.00
7.	Miscellaneous	23,01,662.00	67,176.00	14,77,872.00	1,04,621.00

Source : Field Survey

Out of all units mineral and Chemical industries have high total output and forest based industries have low output. The Engineering industries have low output. The Engineering Industries have moderate output. This trend is good example for the encouragement given by the people or in otherwords this is a good example for growing demand for industries which meet the present demands of the society.

Apart from mineral, Chemical and Engineering Industries, total put per industry is more in agro and Textile industries. The miscellaneous industries have an encouraging trend.

In order to study the, variation between categories and between units regarding value of out put, ANOVA, has been employed and the results indicate that variation is significant at one per cent level (F6, 4.65).

Concluding Remarks

Capital Structure of an industrial unit is an indictor of financial soundness of an industrial unit. Analysis of capital structure of sample units study shows that the overall average of Working Capital, Fixed Capital and Total Capital is Rs. 3,00,433, Rs. 6,24,444, Rs. 9,89,977 respectively. There is inter-category variation with regard to average working capital, average fixed and average total capital. The proportion of Fixed Capital to the Total Capital invested is found to be high (50 per cent and below). There is inter category variation in respect of total output and there is relationship between Capital and Output.

R = Correlation Co-efficient = 0.61.

So we have to reject the Hypothesis, there is relationship between capital and output i.e. higher the capital, the output is high less the capital, the output is also less. And it is observed that there is a positive relation between industrial output and capital.

In order to study the variation between categories and between units, regarding total output ANOVA has been employed the results indicate that the variation is significant at 1% level of significance. F6 = 4.7.

5

Capital and Employment

Introduction

Industrial development has to be viewed in terms of generating higher production and employment. As a part of it, small industrial sector can increase the production of goods and employment to increasing labour force, utilising locally available raw materials and man power resources. Further, promotion of small-scale industrial units generates income in rural areas and benefits the common in the shape of increased availability of goods and services at reasonable prices and better standard of living. The District Industries Centre assists the industrial units in securing all the facilities for the development of these industries.

Employment and production are the important objectives of industrializations. Small-scale industries, considered to be labour intensive, play an important role in the creation of self-employment as well as wage employment. The small-scale industries not only raise per capita income and standard of living of the people but also reduce the disparities among different sectors. The present chapter attempts to examine the employment and production of sample units.

Nature of Production of Sample Units

The nature of production and occupation reflect the volume of employment and the level of income generated.

Production is regular in 55 units (58 per cent) and occasional in the remaining 23 units (24 per cent) and seasonal 17 units (17.9 per cent). The number of units of occasional production (23) exceeds those with seasonal production(17). In Agro Industries, 50 per cent of the units have regular production. In Engineering, 15 units regular, 4 units seasonal and 5 units occasional. In the case of Mineral, 3 units regular, 1 unit occasional. In the case of Chemical 3 units regular, 2 units seasonal, 2 units occasional. In the case of Miscellaneous, 14 units regular, 3 units seasonal, 5 units occasional. The above analysis shows that, in majority of the units of different categories, the production is regular, to the significant there of 60 per cent.

Table 5.1 : Nature of Production of Sample Units
Nature of Production

Sl. No.	Category of Industries	Regular	Seasonal	Occasional	Total
1.	Agro	11	7	5	23
2.	Engineering	15	4	5	24
3.	Forest	5	–	2	7
4.	Textile	4	1	3	8
5.	Mineral	3	–	1	4
6.	Chemical	3	2	2	7
7.	Miscellaneous	14	3	5	22
	Total	**55** **(57.9)**	**17** **(17.9)**	**23** **(24.2)**	**95** **(100)**

Note : Figures in parenthesis are percentage to total
Source : Field Survey

Nature of Occupation of Sample Units

It is observed that the table 5.2. that 57 respondents (60 per cent) the industrial activity is primary as well as exclusively occupation. For the remaining 38 (40 per cent) respondents it is a secondary occupation. For most of the respondents in Agro (14

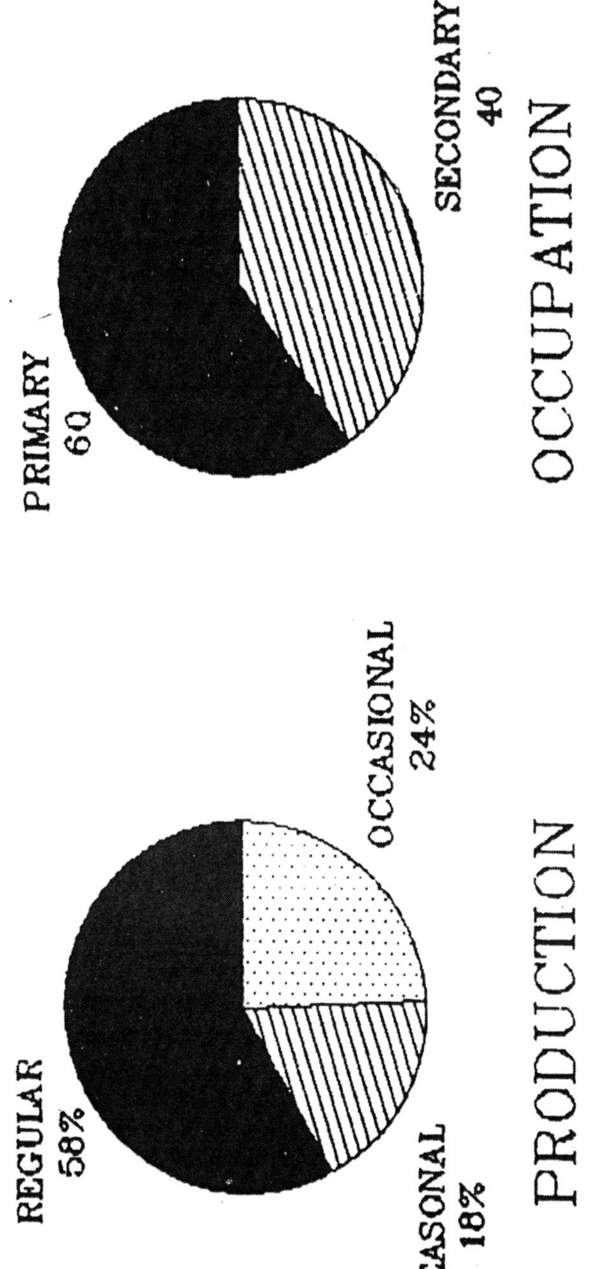

Nature of Production and Occupation of Sample Units

out of 23) and Forest (5 out of 7) the industrial activity is a secondary occupation. For the remaining in Agro (9 out of 23) and Engineering (18 out of 24) and Textile (6 out of 8) and Chemical (5 out of 7) and Miscellaneous (15 out of 22) the industrial activity is a primary occupation. Infact the very seasonally of agriculture may be an important cause for making small-scale industries not only seasonal but also secondary occupation for few. Nature of production and occupation of sample units is also shown in diagram.

Table 5.2 : Nature of Occupation of Sample Units

Sl. No.	*Category of Industries*	*Primary*	*Secondary*	*Total* No. of Units
1.	Agro	9	14	23
2.	Engineering	18	6	24
3.	Forest	2	5	7
4.	Textile	6	2	8
5.	Mineral	2	2	4
6.	Chemical	5	2	7
7.	Miscellaneous	15	7	22
	Total	**57** (60)	**38** (40)	**95** (100)

Note : Figures in parenthesis are percentage to total
Source : Field Survey

Sex-wise Distribution of Workforce and Child Labour

Field data pertaining to employment of male, female and child workers are presented in the Table 5.3.

Out of the total 659 workers in the sample units, 396 (60 per cent) are males, 107 (16 per cent) females and 156 (24 per cent) children. It is observed that the participation of male workers are more in almost all the types of industries, average employment of male workers per unit is 5.2 and it is higher in Chemical (9) Textile (7.3) and mineral (7.3). Female workers are found in almost all the categories of units, except Engineering. Average employment of female workers is (1.8) and it is high in textile (4.8) and Chemical

Table 5.3 :

Sl. No.	*Category of Industry*	*Total*	*Male*	*Female*	*Children*	*Male, Female Children among workers per unit*		
1.	Agro	138	83	25	30	3.6	1.1	1.3
2.	Engineering	120	72	–	48	3.0	–	2.0
3.	Forest	42	25	2	15	3.4	0.3	2.1
4.	Textile	96	58	38	–	7.3	4.8	–
5.	Mineral	48	29	5	14	7.3	1.3	3.5
6.	Chemical	105	63	18	24	9.0	2.6	3.4
7.	Miscellaneous	110	66	19	25	3.0	0.9	1.2
	Total	**659 (100)**	**396 (60)**	**107 (16)**	**156 (24)**	**5.2**	**5.8**	**2.3**
	S.D.					**2.35**	**1.5**	**1.15**
	C.V.					**45%**	**97%**	**60%**

Note : Figures in parenthesis are percentage to total
Source : Field Survey

(2.6). Child workers are found in all the categories of units, except in textile. Average employment of child workers if (2.3) higher in mineral (3.5) and Chemical (3.4). It is diagrammatically shown.

Average employment of male workers per unit is 5.2 and it is higher in Chemical (9), Textile (7.3) and Mineral (7.3). Female workers are found in almost all the categories of units, except Engineering. Average employment of female workers is (1.8) and it is high in Textile (4.8) and chemical (2.6). Child workers are found in all the categories of units, except in textile. Average employment of child workers is (2.3) higher in mineral (3.5) and chemical (3.4). Male S.D. (2.35) C.v. (45 per cent), Female S.D. (1.5). C.V. (97 per cent), children S.D. (1.15) C.V. (60 per cent). For comparing the variability of three salaries calculated the coefficient of variations of each series. The series having greater C.V. that is female (97 per cent) is said to be more variable than the others. The series having lesser C.V. is said to be more consistent than the other that is male C.V. (45 per cent).

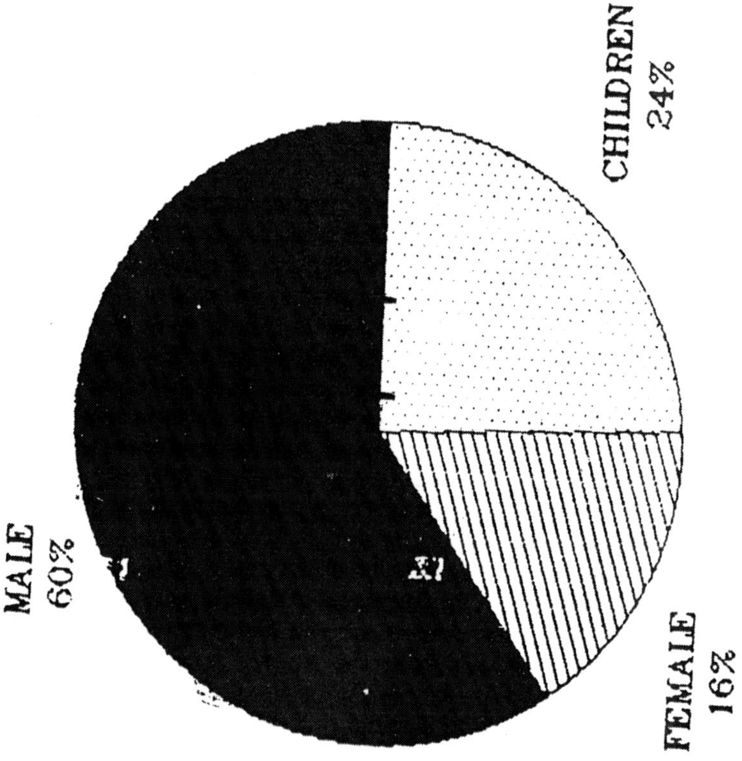

Sex-wise Distribution of Work Force and Child Labour

Composition of Workforce

The average members per unit for the entire sample is 8.7 persons, while the average local workers per unit and the average non-local labours per unit are 6.5 and 2.2 persons respectively. The highest local labour per unit is found in Chemical (11.1), Textile (9.1) and Mineral (8.8.). The highest non-local labour per unit is found in chemical (3.9) and Mineral (3.3). The dispersion of local worker per unit C.V. =43% is lower than non-local per unit C.V. =49%. The series having greater C.V. is said to be more variable than the other and the series having lesser C.V. is said to be more consistent than the other. The data are diagrammatically presented.

Employment Size

The resource use pattern and the size of employment depend on the size of the Small-Scale Industrial units and the mode of production. Data relating to distribution of sample units according to number of persons employed are set out in the Table 5.4.

Table 5.4 :

Sl. No.	*Category of Industry*	*Total No. of workers*	*Local*	*Non-Local*	*Average workers per unit*	*Average No. of local per unit*	*Average No. of non-local per unit*
1.	Agro	138	105	33	6	4.6	1.4
2.	Engineering	120	91	29	5	3.8	1.2
3.	Forest	42	32	10	6	4.6	1.4
4.	Textile	96	73	23	12	9.1	2.9
5.	Mineral	48	35	13	12	8.8	3.3
6.	Chemical	105	78	27	15	11.1	3.9
7.	Miscellaneous	110	84	26	5	3.8	1.2
	Total	**659**	**498**	**161**	**8.7**	**6.5**	**2.2**
	S.D.		**(76)**	**(24)**		**2.8**	**1.06**
	C.V.					**43%**	**49%**

Note : Figures in parenthesis are percentage to total
Source : Field Survey

On the whole, the average employment per unit is 8.7 persons S.D. = 3.8 and C.V. (44 per cent) respectively. The largest average employment is noticed in Chemical (15) followed by the Textile (12) and Mineral (12), Forest (6) and Agro(6), Engineering (5) and Miscellaneous (5) respectively.

An analysis of size structure among the different types of units shows that only one unit in Agro have employed between 10-12 persons, 12 units have employed between 4-6 persons, 5 units have employed between 1-3 persons, 2 units have employed between 13-15 persons. 13 units in Engineering have employed between 4-6 persons. 6 units have employed between 1-3 persons. In Miscellaneous 5 units employed 1-3 persons. In the rest of the units in all categories employment varies between 7-9 and 10-12 persons. Average size of employment in sample units is also diagrammatically shown in figure.

Table 5.5 : Distribution of Sample Units by the Size of Employment

Sl. No.	*Category of Industry*	*1–3*	*4–6*	*7–9*	*10–12*	*13–15*	*Total No. of units*	*Total No. of workers*	*Average workers per unit*
1.	Agro	5	12	3	1	2	23	138	6
2.	Engineering	6	13	3	2	–	24	120	5
3.	Forest	–	4	2	–	1	7	42	6
4.	Textile	–	2	3	2	1	8	96	12
5.	Mineral	–	–	2	2	–	4	48	12
6.	Chemical	1	3	1	2	–	7	105	15
7.	Miscellaneous	5	2	11	2	2	22	110	5
	Total	**17 (18)**	**36 (38)**	**25 (26)**	**11 (12)**	**6 (6)**	**95 (100)**	**659**	**8.7**
	S.D.								3.8
	C.V.								44%

Note : Figures in parenthesis are percentage to total
Source : Field Survey

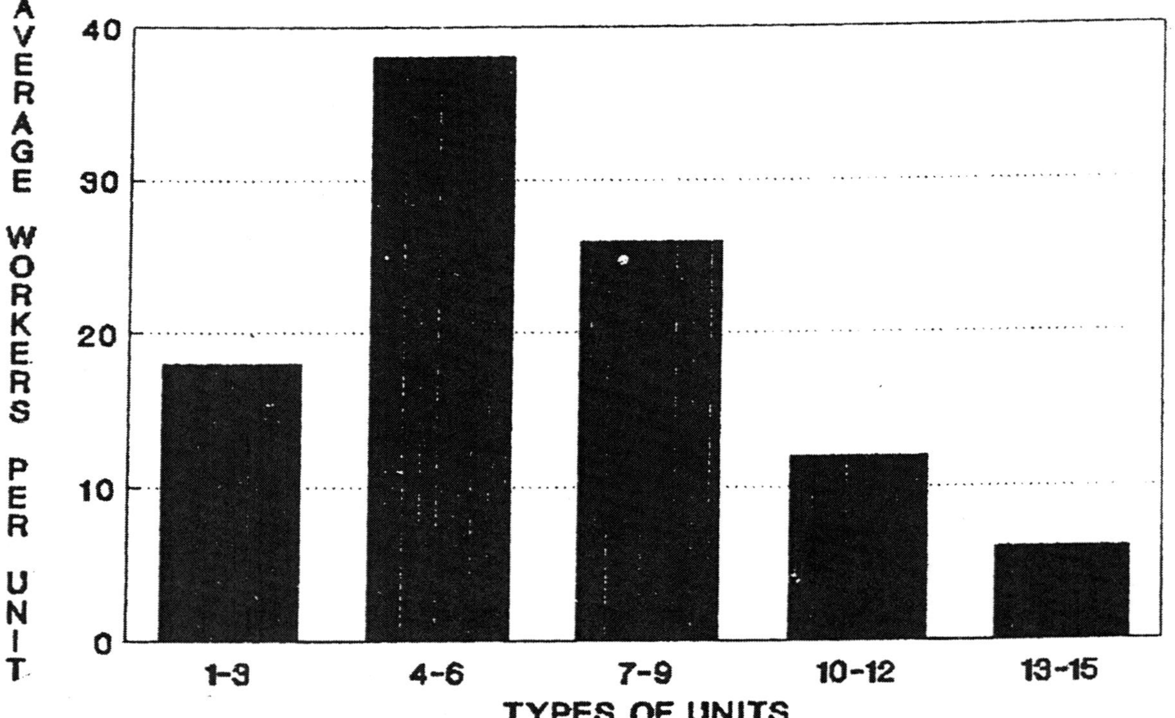

Distribution of Sample Units by Size of Employment

Employment Intensity in Sample Units

Employment in terms of time (man days) indicated, intensity of employment. Average duration of work is 200 man days in a year with S.D. and C.V. of 38.87 days and 19 per cent indicts the extent of dispersion in man days worked. Of the total number of house hold workers (659) 10 per cent work for less than 150 days in a year, 34 per cent between 150-200 days, 42 per cent between 200-300 man days, 12 per cent between 300-325 and two per cent over 325 days. Thus nearly three fourths of the workers work for less than 300 days in a year.

Table 5.6 : Employment Intesity in Sample Units

Sl. No.	*Category of Industry*	*Total No. of workers*	*Person Days worked in a Year (No. of workers)*					
			less than 150	*150–200*	*200–300*	*300–325*	*Above 325*	*Average man days of employees*
1.	Agro	138	–	47	71	19	–	170
2.	Engineering	120	12	48	43	17	–	146
3.	Forest	42	6	16	20	–	–	259
4.	Textile	96	8	24	32	18	14	237
5.	Mineral	48	15	20	9	4	–	171
6.	Chemical	105	–	31	62	12	–	230
7.	Miscellaneous	110	28	35	40	7	–	187
	Total	**659 (100)**	**69 (10)**	**221 (34)**	**277 (42)**	**77 (12)**	**14 (2)**	**200**
	S.D.							**38.87**
	C.V.							**19%**

Note : Figures in parenthesis are percentage to total
Source : Field Survey

The employment is 259 days in Forest based industries, Textile 237 days and Chemical 230 days and these industries provided near full employment. Workers in other types of enterprises are fond to be in a an under employment equilibrium of varying magnitude. The root causes of under employment in small-scale industries are shortage of inputs and inadequate markets.

Value of Output

For comparing the variability of three series calculated the coefficient of variations of each series. The series having greater (capital) C.V. (41 per cent) is said to be more variable than the other that is employment and out put having lesser C.V. and (30 per cent). There is positive relationship between capital and employment. The value of correlation coefficient r = 0.84.

We reject the hypothesis that the employment and capital in various categories of sample units are significant and there is positive relation between employment and capital.

Table 5.7

Sl. No.	*Category of Industries*	*Capital* Rupees in lakhs	*Employ-*	*Production* Value Rs. in lakhs
1.	Agro	21.06	138	26.68
2.	Engineering	11.50	120	24.25
3.	Forest	7.75	42	16.38
4.	Textile	10.00	96	9.76
5.	Mineral	6.07	48	29.42
6.	Chemical	12.18	105	21.63
7.	Miscellaneous	18.05	110	29.92
	Total	**86.61**	**659**	**158.04**
	S.D.	5.00	33.41	6.81
	C.V.	41%	36%	3.0%

Source : Field Survey

Distribution of Sample Units by Value of Annual Production

Output of many industrial units is influenced by its size in terms of capital and workers employed. This is due to unusually high annual output categories Mineral (Rs. in lakhs 7.36 per unit) chemical industries (Rs. in Lakhs 3.09 per unit) Forest based industries (Rs. in lakhs 2.34 per unit) Miscellaneous industries (Rs. in lakhs 1.36 per unit) Agro based industries (Rs. in lakhs 1.16 per unit) and Engineering based industries (Rs. in Lakhs 1.0 per unit). 85 per cent of the sample units have produced average annual output value at over Rs. 1 lakh per unit. Remaining 15 per cent of the sample units have produced average annual output value at over Rs. 2 lakhs per unit. In order to study, the variation between categories and between units regarding value of output ANOVA has been employed and results indicate that the variation to significant. $F_6$4.65

Table 5.8

Sl. No.	Category of Industries	Total no. of units	Less than Rs. 16000	Rs. 20000-60000	Rs. 60000-100000	Rs. 100000- and above	Aver. Annual production Rs. in lakhs	Total Annual production Rs. in lakhs
1.	Agro	23	–	4	8	11	1.16	26.68
2.	Engineering	24	–	5	6	13	1.01	24.25
3.	Forest	7	–	–	3	4	2.34	16.38
4.	Textile	8	–	1	4	3	1.22	9.76
5.	Mineral	4	–	–	–	4	7.36	29.44
6.	Chemical	7	–	–	1	6	3.09	21.63
7.	Miscellaneous	22	1	3	6	12	1.36	29.92
	Total	**95**	**1**	**13**	**28**	**53**	**17.57**	**158.04**
	S.D.						2.10	6.81
	C.V.						84%	30%

Source : Field Survey

Conclusion

Analysis of employment and capital in sample units reveals that there is positive relationship between capital and employment. We reject the hypothesis that the employment and capital in various categories of sample units are significant small-scale Industries are more labour intensive in nature and less capital intensive. The variation between categories and between units regarding value of output is significant.

6

Problems and Prospects of Small-Scale Industrial units

Introduction

The process of promotion and development of small-scale industries in Anantapur District has not been an easy one. All categories of industries suffer from innumerable problems like raw materials, finance, marketing, labour storage, transport and technology. These problems reinforce each other in most of the industries and force the unit into sickness. To study the intensity of each problem in different industries, the Scale Product Value (S.P.V) are presented in the tabular form.

1. Lack of Managerial Experience

Most of the small entrepreneurs rush into their project without doing proper spadework necessary for the success of the project. At the time of initiating their project, they are not in a position to correctly anticipate their financial requirements and the size of market for their production. Small industrial units also lack synchronization between production and marketing. Greater emphasis is put on production, while marketing of the products does not get its due share of the entrepreneurs attention. Besides, entrepreneurs do not possess the necessary marketing intelligence. There is scope for better accounting and financial discipline among entrepreneurs which could enable them to obtain more institutional finance.

Most of the first generation entrepreneurs used to be or use familiarized with the general industrial procedures and practices in various states and at the Centre.

Due to their inability to foreseen such technical procedures and financial obstacles, they are unable to formulate a proper strategy to overcome them. There is a great need for comprehensive, competent and relevant training to the prospective young entrepreneurs.

2. Training and Credit Facilities

About 50% of the small entrepreneurs are not in a position to obtain institutional finance. This indeed, is not healthy sign so for as the growth of small-scale sector is concerned. Generally small entrepreneurs are not in a position to arrange the necessary finance in full from their own resources. As such they are forced to obtain finance from other unorganised financial sector at exorbitant rate of interest.

Banks still follow security-oriented policy, consequently requirements of the entrepreneurs are not fully met. Banks insistence on securities cause great inconvenience besides being a great hurdle to the entrepreneurs. This has stultifying effect on the growth of small industries. Moreover there is no uniformity in the procedure of various Banks. The period for sanction of proposals and interest rates vary from Bank to Bank. The attitude of credit extension to the new entrepreneurs differs from Bank to Bank, even from branch to branch, highlighting the need for attitudinal - orientation of Branch/Branch Managers.

Working capital problems are clearly linked with the marketing of the products. There are inordinate delayed in the payment of Bills by large purchasers, causing immense financial hardships to small entrepreneurs and in certain cases, the complete erosion of their working capital.

Commercial Banks should usher in new innovative enterprising attitudes on the credit extension policies to new entrepreneurs in place of security oriented one. They should at times, be prepared to provide the necessary finance to sick Small-Scale Industries units. As it is, there is a strong need for suitable Legislation to be enacted to protect the small entrepreneurs from the vagaries of delayed payment by the large.

3. Marketing Problems and Lack of Technical Know-how

Nearly 80% of the small entrepreneurs dealing with general market and facing marketing problems while only 20% producing for specified markets. Even they have several problems like delayed payments, proper and timely inspection and fuller utilisation of capacity.

The problems of popularising framed name of the products of Small-Scale Industries quite acute in view of the stiff competition from the established framed names of organised sector. It is beyond the capacity of Small-Scale Industries to afford costly advertisements and there is no arrangement for collective advertisement.

While selecting their products, small entrepreneurs do not bother to gather information regarding the total market for their products; the state of competition in the product line, the prospects of future growth of the market for the product; the position of its substitutes. In the same way, they do not have the necessary scientific knowledge about different alternative technologies and processes available for manufacturing their product, to improve the quality of products and to reduce costs.

There is practically no Agency in the country which can provide regular marketing facility to Small-Scale Industrial Units. A suitable Agency needs to be created to provide regular marketing facility to small entrepreneurs on reasonable basis. Such Agency should not only undertake sales promotion programmes, popularization of framed names by clubbing together a number of Small-Scale Industrial Units producing the same or identical items it should equip itself with up-to-date market information for different products to enable itself to be the competent adviser to the participating entrepreneurs in the selection and diversification of their product lines. Agencies like Department of Small Industries Development Corporation (DSIDC) should be graded upto undertake this job by obtaining the advise of competent marketing consultants. They must ensure that orders are placed equitably amongst entrepreneurs and the benefit of marketing operation to flow to the entrepreneurs. The small-scale industries are an integral part of not only industrial sector, but also of the country's economic structure as a whole. If small-scale industries are properly developed, they can provide a large volume of employment, raise income, standard of living of our people in lower income brackets and bring about a more balanced rural and urban development. For this, technical training and provision for the latest machines and equipment for small-scale sector, market surveys and demand forecasts and their products, provision for working capital and long-term finance liberal terms and managerial training for entrepreneurs are a must to improve the situation. The administrative and procedural delays on the part of Government Agencies connected with small-scale sector and the financial institutions need to be avoided if this sector is to work properly. Bureaucratic red-tapism should be kept at its minimum while dealing with this sector.

Lower educational levels and lack of required technical skills of entrepreneurs did not allow them, either to increase productivity in their units or enable them to pursue the product diversification with the resources available within the district.

Though the industrial goods produced in the district are normally sold out within a month, yet the manufacturer face stuff competition in the market. Many of the units have been engaged in the production of similar products, as such, the industries face inadequate demand for the good produced within the district.

4. Raw Material

The small-scale industries have been facing the problem of raw materials due to periodic scarcity of both indigenous and imported raw materials. The problem of scarcity of raw material is less server in those units depending on the local raw materials than in those an outside sources. The District Industrial Centre provides certain scarce raw materials though the raw material servicing centres and certain other scare raw materials are secured directly from the producing agencies with the recommendation of District Industrial Centre. Most of the entrepreneurs have reported that the materials supplied through Raw Material Servicing Centres are not supplied regularly. Sometimes, supply took more than 3 months.

5. Market

The major underlying causes of marketing problems are

poor quality of the product high prices, lack of knowledge of the market and lack of distributive contacts. Though the District Industrial Centre recommends various institutions to provide marketing assistance to small-scale industries, marketing assistance is provided only to the furniture manufacturing units, electrical parts manufacturing units and chemical industrial. Moreover marketing assistance takes such a lot of time to reach the units, some of them meanwhile may fall sick by the time they get marketing assistance.

6. Labour

Labour problem is common in manufacturing of parts requiring, skilled labours. Few entrepreneurs attended the training programmes conducted by the Andhra Pradesh Productivity Council for improvement of managerial abilities and upgradation of skills. The entrepreneurs were satisfied with District Industries Centres move in arranging their training programmes.

7. Transport

Transport becomes a problem when the industrial establishment is far away from the source of inputs. Procurement of the finished products to market also poses a serious problem due to inadequate transport facilities. Provision of transport facilities is necessary for the growth of any sector industry.

8. Storage

The problem of storage of inputs and outputs also need proper alterations. If they produce more goods, they are not able to keep the finished products in a right place due to lack of storage facilities. Further, this lack of facilities forces them to purchases raw-material whenever they are in need and at higher prices. Besides this, they are forced to dispose of their products at cheaper prices because of inadequate storage facilities.

Raw Material Problems of Small-Scale Industries in Anantapur District

It is observed from the present study that the availability of raw material does not seem to be a problem for 59 units (62%) of sample units. Out of 36 units the problem is very serious in the case of 12 units (13%) and serious for 24 units (25%) of units. All the respondents of the Forest Textile and Miscellaneous reported that procuring raw material was not a problem. 5 units out of 23 Agro based, 4 output 7 chemical based industries reported availability of raw material was a very serious problems. For the remaining respondents, 8 out of 23 in Agro 9 out of 24 in Engg., 3. Out of 7 in Forest, 4 out of 8 in Textile, 1 out of 4 in Mineral, 1 out of 7 in Chemical, it was a serious problem, 10 out of 23 in Agro, 11 out of 24 in Engg., 4 out of 7 in Forest, 3 out of 8 in Textile, 2 out of 4 in Mineral, 4 out of the 7 in Chemical and Miscellaneous, it was not a serious problem.

Financial Problems of Small-Scale Industries in Anantapur District

Finance appears to be a one of the several problems for the small-scale industries located in Anantapur District of the present study. It is evident from the table that out of the total 95 units 47 (48%) units reported finance as a major problem. 48 units (52%) expressed finance as not a big question. 14 units (13%) reported finance as a very serious problem, the time taken in the sanction of loans and their actual disbursement was also stated to be disproportionately long.

Power Problems of Small-Scale Industries in Anantapur District

Power appears to be a major restraint for the small-scale industries located in Anantapur District of the present study. It is evident from the table no. 6.1 that out of 95 units, 73 units (77%) reported Power as bottleneck and among them 48 units (51%) expressed power as a very serious problem. As 25 units (26%) reported power as a serious problem. Only 22 units (23%) it was not a constraint.

Marketing Problem of Small Industries in Anantapur District

Marketing appears to be a major problem for sample units of Anantapur District as 76 units (80%) reported positively in this regard. Only 20%) 19 units out of 95 units, it is not a problem. 12 units out of 23 in Agro, 11 units out of 24 in Engineering, 2 units out of 7 in forest, 1 unit out of 8 in Textile, 2 units out of 4 in Mineral, 2 units out of 7 in Chemical, 8 units out of 22 in Miscellaneous encountered marketing as a very serious problem. 7 units out of

23 in Agro, 9 units out of 24 in Engineering, 4 units out of 7 in Forest, 6 units out of 8 in Textiles, 2 units out of 4 in mineral, 3 units out of 7 in Chemical, 7 units out of 22 in Miscellaneous have been experiencing marketing as a serious problem. 4 units each out of 23 in Agro and out of 24 in Engineering 1 unit each in Forest and Textile 2 units in Chemical, 7 units in Miscellaneous, marketing problem does not seem to be a big problem.

Storage Problem of Small-Scale Industries in Anantapur District

Only 17 units (18%), 22 units (23%) of the present study in Anantapur district storage is a serious constraint as they undertake production in anticipation of demand 56 units (59%) it does not appear to be a problem at all.

Transport and Labour Problem of Small-Scale Industries in Anantapur District

In Anantapur District, transportations is a problem to 18 unit (19%) falling under the categories of Agro units out of 23, 4 units out of the 24 in Engg., 10 units in each Forest and Textile, 2 units each in Mineral, Chemical and Miscellaneous for the rest of the sample units, it does not appear to be a problem at all.

The problem of labour, as such is not a very serious one. This is evident from the fact that out of 95 units of the present study in Anantapur District only 29 units (30%) expressed it as a serious problem. This problem is expressed only in the case of Agro, Engg., Mineral, Chemical and Miscellaneous. For 66 units (70%) labour is not a constraint. Particularly in the matter of availability of skilled labour force, it can be concluded that existing state of affairs is far from satisfactory.

Prospects

4507 Small-Scale Industries have been established in Anantapur District with the capital investment in Rs. 36.58 crores, providing employment to 28,113 persons. There is very good scope for further establishment of small-scale industries in the District. Intensive and concerted efforts are being made for the rapid industrial development, by organising intensive industrial companies in the District. 28 large and medium-scale industries, with an Investment of Rs. 121.13 crores are providing employment to 9,413 persons.

Table 6.1 : Operational Problems of Sample Units

Sl. No.	*Category*	*Total No. of units*	*Raw Material*			*Finance*			*Power*			*Marketing*			*Storage*			*Transport*			*Labour*		
			VS	*S*	*NS*	*VS*	*S*	*NS*	*VS*	*S*	*NS*	*VS*	*S*	*NS*	*VS*	*S*	*NS*	*VS*	*S*	*NS*	*VS*	*S*	*NS*
1.	Agro	23	5	8	10	2	11	10	11	8	4	12	7	4	6	4	13	1	5	17	2	4	17
2.	Engineering	24	4	9	11	4	9	11	13	5	6	11	9	4	6	3	15	2	2	20	3	3	18
3.	Forest	7	–	3	4	2	2	3	3	2	2	2	4	1	–	3	4	–	1	6	–	3	4
4.	Textile	8	–	4	3	1	2	5	3	2	3	1	6	1	2	1	5	–	1	7	–	3	5
5.	Mineral	4	1	1	2	1	2	1	2	1	1	2	2	–	1	2	1	–	2	2	1	2	1
6.	Chemical	7	2	1	4	1	4	2	4	2	1	2	3	2	2	3	2	1	1	5	2	2	3
7.	Miscellaneous	22	-	-	22	3	3	16	12	5	5	8	7	7	–	6	16	–	2	20	1	3	18
		95	**12**	**26**	**57**	**14**	**33**	**48**	**48**	**25**	**22**	**38**	**38**	**19**	**17**	**22**	**56**	**4**	**14**	**77**	**9**	**20**	**66**
		100	(13)	(25)	(62)	(13)	(35)	(52)	(51)	(26)	(23)	(40)	(40)	(20)	(18)	(23)	(59)	(4)	(15)	(81)	(10)	(20)	(70)

Note : Figures in parenthesis are percentages to total.

V.S. = Very Serious, S = Serious, NS = Not Serious.

In order to know the intensity of the problem of sample units, scale product values have been computed and results are presented in Table 6.2

Table 6.2 : Intensity of Problems of Sample Units

Sl. No.	*Problem*	*Very Serious*	*Serious*	*Not Serious*	*Scale Product Value*
1.	Raw Materials	12 (13%)	24 (25%)	59 (65%)	48.09
2.	Finance	14 (13)	33 (35)	48 (52)	14.07
3.	Power	48 (51)	25 (26)	22 (23)	32.61
4.	Marketing	38 (40)	38 (40)	19 (20)	32.61
5.	Storage	17 (18)	22 (23)	56 (59)	8.54
6.	Transport	4 (4)	14 (15)	97 (81)	2.38
7.	Labour	9 (10)	20 (20)	66 (70)	5.16

SAource : Field Survey

The results show that Raw Material is the major constraint for the sample units as revealed by scale product value (S.P.V. 48.09). Marketing and power is the next important problems (S.P.V. 32.61) it is follow by finance (S.P.V. 14.07), storage (S.P.V.) 8.54) labour (S.P.V. 5.6) transport (S.P.V. 2.38)

Reasons for Slow Growth of Entrepreneurs in the District

1. The district accounts for low percentage of educated people and even among the educated most of the people do not have technical skills to pursue industrial ventures in the district.

2. It is said that the manager of the nationalised commercial banks have been adopting rigid banking procedure in extend-

ing financial assistance to SSI units in the district. The Managers of the banks have been insisting upon the entrepreneurs to produce a surety to avail themselves of the bank finance. This has been retraining many entrepreneurs who want to start industrial units in the district but fail to produce a surety to bankers get financial assistance owing to their poor asset position.

So, in the interest of accelerated industrial development of the backward areas, credit must be made available on more liberal terms to entrepreneurs who have at present incapable of availing themselves of credit facilities because of certain rigidities.

Concluding Remarks

The development of Small-Scale Industrial units is constrained by the presence of certain operational problems and this tendency prevents in sample units in varying degrees. Since independence, through Industrial Policy Resolutions the Government has been aiming at ensuring decentralised cottage, village and small-scale industrial sectors to acquire sufficient vitality to be self supporting. However, the Small-Scale Industrial units continue to suffer from variety of problems as the Government policy towards them appears to be protectionist rather than promotional. In recent times certain schemes have been launched to promote and modernise small-scale industrial units.

The effect of these efforts seems to be marginal and the Small-Scale Industrial units are still in the grip of various circle of the problems leakage in delivery of raw materials and credit and provision of inadequate socio-economic infrastructure besides techno economic services.

It is evident from what is discussed above that all small-scale industrial units are afflicted with a multitude of problems. It is true that there are some variations in the nature and extent of the problems experienced by the different small-scale industrial groups. There are again some variations among the different sample units with in the same industry group also in the matter of the extent and nature of the problem with which they are confronted with. It is high time, that feasible ways and means have to be found out to over come these problems without any further loss of time. It is only then that we can visualise a bright and prosperous future for the Small-Scale Industries in Anantapur District.

7

Summary of Findings and Conclusions

Introduction

"Economic Development of a country depends upon the utility of its people to use new techniques which ensure high production industry not only produces the inputs required for the introduction of modern science and technology but it also helps to produce an army of people with technicians, accountants, economists and so on, who help to use these inputs with dynamic effects on economic development".[1]

There is a positive relationship between industrialization and economic development. "In countries like India and Japan with a high ratio of population to natural resources and in particular to land, manufacturing industry represents virtually the only hope of greatest increasing labour products and raising levels of living."[2]

It would be appropriate for an under developing country to concentrate investible resources initially on the development of agriculture sector and other simple industrial activities which do not absorb much capital.

Small-Scale Industries in India, Policies Programmes and Performance

The small-scale industries have enough scope to exploit available local resources such as small savings, raw materials, skilled and unskilled labour. Further, they generate income for consumption of wage goods and provide employment to unemployed persons. So, it is necessary to allot public sector investment for development of infrastructural facilities and provide incentives through development programme for setting up of small industries.

The Industrial Policy Resolution (1948) stressed the need for development of small-scale industries. The objectives of the policy are

(1) to establish a social order where justice and equality of opportunities could be assured.

(2) to raise the standard of living of the people through exploitation of talents and available resources of the country,

(3) to accelerate production to meet the needs of the growing population and

(4) to provide more and more opportunities for employment.[3] This policy was in force up to 1956.

During the First Five Year-Plan, a major steps taken for the development of village and small industries was the establishment of small-scale industries Boards to advise and assist the Central Government in the formation of programmes for development of handloom industry, Khadi and village industries, small-scale industries, handicrafts, sericulture and coir, International Team of experts was invited by the Government of India in 1953 to study the problems of small-scale industries. The team recommended the establishment of Regional Small Industries Service Institute and accordingly four such Institutes were set up at Bombay, Ca'cutta, Madurai and Faridabad with branch units in Uttar Pradesh, Bihar, Andhra Pradesh and Travancore - Cochin. These Institutes provide various kinds of technical services to village and techniques of production, technical advise and assistance in the utilisation of the local raw materials". The programme of work of the Small-Scale Industries Board follows largely the lines indicate in the Report of the International Planning Team. The main part of the programme was the establishment of a number of Institutes for organisation, technical servicing and business connecting and marketing assistance.

Industrial Estates

The Industrial Estates Programme was started in 1955 following the recommendations of the International Planning Team. Under this programme, suitable sites with all the facilities such as water, electricity, transport, steam, communications, Banks, Post-office, raw materials depots, canteens, watches and ward, First-Aid etc., are to be provided so as to create the necessary climate for the development of small industries. The main objectives of the industrial estates programme are:

1. To shift the small-scale industries from congested areas to industrial estates with a view to increasing this productivity.
2. To achieve decentralised industrial development in small town and villages and,
3. To assist ancillary industries in the townships surrounding major industrial under-takings, both in the Public and Private sector. The Government of India had given a big boost under different Five Year Plans by encouraging the establishment of Industrial Estates in the country.

Present Study

Area-specific microlevel studies will be useful to understand the problems and prospects of small-scale industries pertaining to different regions in the country, particularly backward region. Against this background, the present study is attempted covering Anantapur District of Andhra Pradesh with the focus on capital, employment and operational problems and prospects of sample units.

Agriculture is the main occupation of the people of Anantapur District as about 70 per cent of the working population depends on agriculture, either directly or indirectly.

There are 28 large and medium-scale industries in the District with a capital investment of Rs. 121.13 crores and providing employment to about 9413 people. The District's valuable resources of minerals lare Barytes, Limestone, Steatite, white clay, white shale, iron ore and Dolamite.

The District Industries Centre was started in 1978 for the promotion of small-scale tiny village and cottage industries. There has been a steady increase in small-scale industries.

Profile of Sample Units

For the purpose of the study, 95 units covering screen categories from the District were selected using simple random sampling procedure.

Regarding location, 70.5 per cent of the units are favorable to the present industrial location. Whereas 29.5 per cent are feeling that the present industrial location is not suitable to carry their industrial activity.

45 per cent of the units are producing goods only to meet the local District Markets and rest 55 per cent produce goods to meet local as well as outside District markets. Large number of units under the categories of all local as well as outside District Market.

The rate of literacy among the sample respondents as 24.3 per cent reported that they cannot read and write in any language. In the remaining 51.58 per cent also only 24.3 per cent respondents have college education and the rest have formal schooling. The rate of illiteracy is high in Agroi-based and Miscellaneous.

Literacy is high in care of mineral based industries and Chemical based (100 per cent) industries followed by respondents belonging to Agro-based industries is (70 per cent) Engineering based (80 per cent), Forest base industries (71 per cent), Miscellaneous (73 per cent). They can read and write. As a result most of them are literates and that is why a high rate of employment is found among the sample small-scale industries.

Employment and Capitals

55 units are carrying on the present industrial activity as regular, 23 units as occasional and 17 units as seasonal, the production activity is regular in majority of the units of different categories. For 57 respondents the industrial activity in primary while for the 38 respondents it is secondary.

The average employment per unit is 8.7 persons and it is high in Chemical (15 persons) and low in the case of Engineering and Miscellaneous (5 persons).

Out of the total 659 workers engaged in sample units 396 (60 per cent) are males, 107 (16 per cent) females and 156 (24 per cent) children. The average male workers per unit is 2.35 and the highest is found in chemical, (9.0 per unit) and lowest in Engineering and

Miscellaneous (3.0 per unit). The average female workers per unit and child workers per unit is 5.8 and 2.3 respectively and Textile has the highest average female workers per unit is (4.8). Female employment and child labour are also wide spread among types of industries characterized by a higher degree of labour intensity.

Average local worker per unit is (6.5 persons) and non local worker per unit is (2.2 persons).

The average total annual production of the sample units is Rs. 2.51 in lakhs per annum. The highest average value of annual production per unit is observed in Mineral (Rs. 7.36) in Chemical (Rs. 3.09), Forest (Rs. 2.34) and Miscellaneous (Rs. 1.36) while the lowest, in the case of Engineering (Rs. 1.01) industries. The variation between categories and between units insignificant.

The relationship between employment and capital in sample unit is positive.

Capital Structure

26 per cent of the units have working capital less than Rs. 5,000. 13 per cent of the units posses the working capital in the range of Rs. 5,000- Rs. 10,000. 16 per cent of units operate with working capital in the range of Rs. 30,000-Rs. 60,000. 19 per cent of units operate with working capital Rs. 60,000 - Rs. 1,00,000 and above. Variation in fixed capital in found par higher than working capital. The production of working capital in the total capital inverted is less in all the categories.

In the total investment of the sample units, 36.2 per cent is met by the own funds, 29.2 per cent from banks, 28.9 per cent from State Finance Corporation the remaining 6.2 per cent of financial assistance from other sources.

The capital intensity as measured by capital output ratio is lower is seven categories of industries the over all ratio of fixed capital to out put is 0.216 that of total capital to output is 1.03.

Problems and Prospects

Small-Scale Industries in Anantapur District are inter alia be set with diversity of problems like raw materials, finance, marketing, labour, storage and transport. Raw Material in the main constraint (S.P.V = 48.09) of the sample units. Power (S.P.V. = 32.61) Marketing (S.P.V. = 32.61), Finance (S.P.V. 14.07), Storage (S.P.V.

8.54), Labour (S.P.V. =5.16) and Transport (S.P.V. = 2.38) came in that order. It is true that there are some variations in the nature and extent of the problems experienced by the different small-scale industrial groups.

Concluding Remarks

Analysis of employment in sample units reveals that Female employment and child labour are also widespread in all types of industries. The average employment in sample units is 8.7. The average production from industrial activity of sample units is Rs. 2.51 lakhs. The study reveals that there is a positive relationship between employment and capital, positive, relationship between capital and production. Hence, we reject the hypothesis.

References

1. Government of India (1936), Report of Karva Committee on village and small Industries, New Delhi, Planning Commission, 1956. Government of India (1968) Report of Ashok Mehta Commission, New Delhi, Department of Industrial Development, 1966.
2. Malhotra, R., (1965), Governor of R.B.I. 19-7-1985 proceedings of the seminal sponsored by Government of Karnataka, Bank Finance for Rural Artisans and Rural Industries 19th July, p.
3. Ram K. Vepa, (1969), Industrial Development in Andhra Pradesh M. Seshchalam and company, Masulipatnam P. 138.

Bibliography

Books

Abdul Aziz, *The Rural Poor : Problems and Prospects*, Ashish Publishing House, New Delhi, (1983).

Akram, S., *Development of Small-Scale Industries in Bihar*, Delhi, Capital Publishing House, 1984.

Alexander, R.J., *A Primer to Economic Development*, The Macmillan and Co. Ltd., London, 1962.

Anderson Dennis, *Financing Small-Scale Industry and Agriculture in Developing Countries*, World Bank Staff Working Paper, 519, Washington, 1982.

Balasa, *The Process of Industrial Development and Alternative Development Strategy*, World Bank Staff Working Papers, 1980.

Bama, D.S., "*New Strategy for Industrial Development of Flood and Drought Prone Area*" Hauz Khas Enclave, New Delhi, 1970.

Baner, P.F. and Yemey, B.S., "*The Economics of under-developed countries*, Cambridge University Press, London, 1965.

Bhattacharya, S. N., "*Development of Industrial Backward Area" (The Indian Style) Metropolitan*, Pragati Press, through V.R.N. Composing Agency, Delhi, 1981.

Bhojendra Nath Banerjee, *Industry Agriculture and Rural Development, B.R. Publishing Corporation*, New Delhi (1987).

Chowdary Muktar Singh, *Cottage and Small-Scale Industries*, Kitabistan Publishers, Allahabad (1947).

Coldar B.N., *Productivity Growth in Indian Industry*, New Delhi, Allied Publishers Pvt. Ltd., 1986.

Cykor G., *Strategies for Industrialisation in Developing Countries*, C. Hurst and Co., London (1974).

Desai Vasanth, *Problems and Prospects of Small-Scale Industries*, Himalaya Publishing House, Bombay, 1983.

Dhar P.N. and Lyndall H.T., *The Role of Small Enterprises in Indian Economic Development*, Asia Publishing House, Bombay, 1961.

Dobb, *Economic Growth and under-developed Countries*, London, 1953.

Everett E. Magen, *Hand Book for Industry Studies*, Asia Publishing House, New Delhi, 1959.

Farooque Q.H., *Small-Scale and Cottage Industries as a Means of Providing Letter Opportunities for Labour in India*, Agra University, 1958.

Godbole M.D., *Industrial Dispersal Policies*, Bombay, Himalaya Publishing House, 1979.

George Rosen, *Industrial Change in India*, Asia Publishing House, New Delhi, 1959.

Government of India, *A Hand Book : Extension Services for Rural Industrial Development*, New Delhi, Development Commissioner, Small-Scale Industries, 1980.

Government of India, *Small-Scale Industries in India—Policies Programmes and Institutional Support*, New Delhi, Development Commissioner, Small-Scale Industries, 1982.

Gunnar Myrdal, *Economic theory and under-developed Regions*, Vora and Co., Publishing (P) Ltd., Bombay, 1958.

Hoffman W.G., *The Growth of Industrial Economics*, Oxford University Press, 1958.

KSSR, *A Survey of Research in Economics*, Vol. V, Allied Publishers, New Delhi, 1975.

Industrial Development Bank of India, Industrial Development of Backward Areas, Bombay, IDBI, 1981.

Iyer Ganapati E.V., *Indian Industrial Development and its Problems*, Ganapati Trans west, Bangalore, Association Pvt. Ltd., 1986.

Isard W., *Methods of Regional Analysis, An Introduction to Regional Science*, Wiley New York, 1960.

Iyer Krishna T.N., *Guideline for Financing of Small-Scale Industries, A Hand Book for Bankers*, Bombay, Sevak Prakasam, 1980.

Jain P.C., *Industrial Problems of India*, Kitabistan, Allhabad, 1942.

James C., Van Horne, *Financial Management in Policy*, Prentice Hall of India, New Delhi, 1974.

Joshi, Navin, C., *Cottage and Small-Scale Industry in India*, Suneja Book Centre, New Delhi, 1956.

Kaur Kula Winder, *Strucutre of Industries in India*, New Delhi, Deep and Deep Publications, 1983.

Killy P., *Small Scale Industry in Kenya*, IBRD (Mimeo), Development Economics Department, 1981.

Kilby P. (Ed.), *Entrepreneurship and Economic Development*, New York, The Free Press, 1971.

Kirpatrick, C.H. and N. Lee and F.I. Nixson, *Industrial Structure and Policy in less Developed Countries*, New Delhi, Heritage Publishers, 1985.

Kuznets, Simon, *Modern Economic Growth*, New Delhi, Oxfords I.B.H. Publishing Co., 1965.

Lakshman Rao V., *Economic Development of Andhra Pradesh*, B.R. Publishing Corporation, Delhi, 1985.

Little Ian, M.D. et al., *Small Manufacturing Enterprises—A Comparative Study of India and other Economics*, World Bank, Oxford University Press, 1987.

Lydall H.F., *Economic Development*. Asia Publishing House, 1960.

Malenbaum W., *Prospects of Indian Development*. George Allen and Unwin, London, 1961.

Mandelbaum K., *Industrialisation of Backward Area*, Basil Blackwell, Oxford, 1961.

Manohar U. Desh Pande, *Entrepreneurship of Small-Scale Industries*, New Delhi, Deep and Deep Publications, 1982.

Mehta M.M., *Structure of Indian Industries*, Popular Book Depot, Bombay, 1955.

Mehta, S.S., *Productivity, Production Function and Technical Change: A Survey of Some Indian Industries*, New Delhi, Concept Publishing House, 1980.

Mehta, M.M., *Structure of Indian Industries*, Bombay, Popular Book Depot, 1961.

Menon, K.S.V., *Development of Backward Areas through Incentives—An Indian Experiment*, New Delhi, Vidya Vahini, 1979.

Misra S.N. and Kaushal Sharma, *Organisational Requirements of Village and Small-Scale Industries*—A Case Study of Alwar District of Rajasthan, Delhi, Mittal Publicatins, 1986.

Mohan Lal, *Rural Indsutrialisation and Regional Development*, New Delhi, Deep and Deep Publications, 1987.

Muniratnam Naidu K, *Industrial Development of Andhra Pradesh* (A Studies in Regional Planning), Sri Venkateswara University Press, Tirupathi.

Nau Nihal Singh, *Scientiic Management of Small-Scale Industries*, Bombay, Lalvani Publishing House, 1970.

Nannjudan S., *Economic Research for Small Industry Development*, Stanford Research Institute, California, 1960.

NCAER, *Survey of Backward District of Andhra Pradesh*, New Delhi, 1970.

NCACER, *Under-utilisation of Industrial Capacity*, New Delhi, 1966.

Myrdal, Gunnar, *International Economy*, New York, Harper and Brothers, 1956.

Pandey T. M., *Capital Strucutre and the Cost of Capital*, Vikas Publishing House, New Delhi, (1985).

Patwardhan V.S., *Role of Small-Scale Industries in the Process of Puna and Aurangabad Districts of Maharastra*, Puna, Grokhale Institute of Politics and Economics, 1985.

Ramakrishna Sharma, *Industrial Development of Andhra Pradesh*, Himalaya Publishing House, Bombay, 1982.

Ram Dawar, *Institutional Finance to Small-Scale Industries Hire-Purchase Finance for Plant and Machinery*, New Delhi, Deep and Deep Publications, 1986.

Ramesh P. Sinha, *Some Problems of Small-Scale Industry*, New Delhi, Janaki Prakashan, 1985.

Rosen, George, *Industrial Changes in India*, Bombay, Asia Publishing House, 1957.

Robinson E.A.G. (ed.), *Backward Areas in Advanced Countries*, MacMillan, 1969.

Sadak H., *Industrial Development in Backward Regions in India*, Allhabad, Chugh Publication, 1986.

Sandesara J.C., *Efficacy of Incentives for Small Industries : Principal Findings of the Bombay, Hyderabad and Jaipur Surveys and their Explanations and Implications*, Bombay, Industrial Development Bank of India, 1982.

Sarma R.K., *Industrial Development of Andhra Pradesh. A Regional Analysis*, Bombay, Himalaya Publishing House, 1982.

Sen A.K., *Employment, Technology and Development*, Oxford Clarendon Press, 1975.

Sharma S.V.S., *Small Entrepreneurial Development in Some Asian Countries—A Comparative Study*, New Delhi, Hight and Life Publishers, 1979.

Singh A.K., *Patterns of Regional Development—A Comparative Study*, New Delhi, Sterling Publishrs Pvt. Ltd., 1981.

Singh N.K., *Industrial Progress and Economic Growth*, New Delhi, Classical Publishing Company, 1982.

Small Industry Extension Training Institute, Capital Requirements of Small Industry, Hyderabad, SIET Institute, 1974.

Stalay, Engene and Richard Morse, *Modern Small Industry for Developing Countries*, New York, McGraw Hill Book Company, 1965.

Takafusa Nakamura, *Economic Development of Modern Japan*, Japan, Ministry of Foreign Affairs, 1985.

Tandar B.C., *Pattern and Technique of India's Economic Development*, Allhabad, Chugh Publications, 1977, Vol. 1.

Tarum T.N.S., *Small-Scale Industries and India's Economic Development*, New Delhi, Deep and Deep Publications, 1986.

Tyaguneuk O.V.L., *Industrialistion of Development Countries*, Progress Publishers, Moscow, 1973.

United Nations, *Progress and Problem of Industrialisation to Under-developed Countries*, 1955.

Upadhayaya K.K., *Financing of Industrial Growth in a Developing Region*, Allahabad, Chugh Publications, 1980.

Vepa Ram, K., *Small Indsutry : Challenges of the Eighties*, New Delhi, Vikas Publsihing House, 1983.

Vepa Ram, K., *How to Succeed in Small Indsutry*, New Delhi, Vikas Publishing House, 1984.

Visweswaraiah Sir, M., *Prosperity through Industry.*

World Bank, *Employment and the Development of Small Enterprises*, A Sector Policy Paper, February, 1980.

World Bank, *Employment and Development of Small Enterprises, Section Policy Paper*, 1978.

Reports

Andhra Pradesh Industrial and Technical Consultancy Organisation Limited, Report on Rehabilitation of Sick Units in the Small Sector, *APITCO, February, 1986.*

Asian and Pacific Development Centre (Kualalumpur, Malaysia), Case Studies on Rural Non-Farm Activities in Kanyakumari District, Tamil Nadu and Midnapore District, West Bengal, Hyderabad, SIET Institute, May, 1984.

Asian Productivity Organisation, Productivity through Consultancy in Small Industries Enterprises, APO Tokyo 107, Japan, 1974.

Centre for Monetoring Indian Economy, Economic Intelligence Service, Basic Statistics relating to the Indian Economy, Bombay, Centre for Monetoring Indian Economy, September, 1989.

Development Commissioner, Small-Scale Industries, Self-employment Programme for Educated Unemployed Youth—An Evaluation Study in two Districts of Andhra Pradesh, New Delhi Planning Commission, January, 1989.

———, All India Report on the Census of Small-Scale Industries, Vol. I, New Delhi, Planning Commission, 1976.

———, Proceedings of 3rd All India District Industries Centres Conference, New Delhi, Ministry of Industry, July, 15–16, 1986.

District Industries Centre, Report of the Action Plan for Industrial Development, Five Year Plan (1990–93) Anantapur.

District Planning Office : The Hand Book of Statistics, Anantapur District, Anantapur (1990–91).

Government of Andhra Pradesh, Statistical Abstract of Andhra Pradesh, Hyderabad, Bureau of Economics and Statistics (1990–91).

———, Agenda Notes, Regional Conference of District Industries Centres at Vijay Nadu on the West; Krishna on the North and River Gundlakamma and Parts of Kamma Nadu on the South (Fig. 6).

———, Agenda Notes, State Level Conference of General Managers of District Indsutries centres, Directorate of Industries, June, 1982.

Government of Andhra Pradesh, Report of the Gramodaya Scheme, prepared by Andhra Pradesh Productivity Council on behalf of Commissioner for Special Employment Scheme, Hyderabad, Commissioner of Industries, 1983.

———, Agenda Notes, Conference of General Managers District Industries Centres, Telangana, Region, Hyderabad, Commissioner of Industries, 1984.

———, Guidelines for setting up Small-Scale Industries in Andhra Pradesh, Commissioner of Industries, 1984.

———, Report of the District Industries Centres in Andhra Pradesh, Directorate of Industries (Brief Resume 1978–79 and 1979–80).

Government of India, First Five Year Plan (1950–55), New Delhi, Planning Commission.

———, Report of the Village and Small-Scale Industries Committee, Second Five Year Plan, New Delhi, Planning Commission.

Government of India, First Five Year Plan (1950–55), New Delhi Planning Commission.

———, Report of the Village and Small-Scale Industries Committee, Second Five Year Plan, New Delhi, Planning Commission, October, 1955.

———, Fourth Five Year Plan (1969–74), New Delhi, Planning Commission.

———, Draft Five Year Plan (1978–83), New Delhi, Planning Commission.

———, Statement on Industrial Policy, New Delhi, Planning Commission, July 23, 1980.

———, Evaluation Study of Rural Industries Projects, New Delhi, Planning Commission (PE.O.), 1978.

———, Small-Scale Industries in India, Hand Book Statistics, New Delhi, 1985.

———, Report of the Woking Group on Indentification of Backward Area, New Delhi, Planning Commission.

———, Report of the Working Group—Fiscal and Financial Incentives for Starting Industries in Backward Areas, Development Commissioner (SSI), Ministry of Industrial Development, 1969.

———, Development Programme for Small-Scale Industries in Backward Areas, Report of the Committee to Evolve a Strategy(Chairman, P.C. Naik), Government of Idnia, 1976.

Government of India, First All India Workshop : General Managers of DICs, New Delhi, Development Commissioner, Small-Scale Industries, 1979.

———, District Industries Centres : Gleanings from two Case Studies, Hyderabad, SIET Institute, February, 1989.

———, District Industries Centre Scheme : A Overview upto January 31, 1984, New Delhi, Development Commissioner, Small-Scale Industries, 1984.

———, Annual Survey of Industries, India for Various Years, New Delhi, Central Statistical Organisation.

———, Physical Achievements of DIC Programme (6th Plan, 1980-81—1984-85), An Appraisal, New Delhi, Development Commissioner (Small-Scale Industries).

Government of Maharastra, Report of the Fact Finding Committee on Regional Imbalances in Maharastra, Bombay, July, 1984.

Indian Institute of Management, Evaluation of DIC Programme in Andhra Pradesh, Bangalore, May, 1988.

Industrial Development Bank of India, Reports on Development Banking in India, Bombay (Various years) 1982-83 to 1987-88.

International Labour Organisation (ILO), Strategies for Employment Promotion—An Evaluation of Four Inter-agency Employment Missions, Eneva, I.L.O., 1973.

Articles

Antonio Vazquez Barquero, Small Industry in Rural Areas. The Spanish Experience since the Beginning of this Century. Paper presented at 8th World Economic Congress of International Economic Association. New Delhi (1986).

Banerjee M.K., District Industrial Centres : Some Comments, *Yojana*, September, 16, 1978.

Banerji A., Productivity Growth and Factor Substitution in Indian Manufacturing, *Indian Economic Review, April, 1971.*

Bhalla A.S., Innovations and Small Producers in Developing Countries, *Economic and Political Weekily, February 25, 1989*, pp. M2–M14.

Bhatt V.V., Entrepreneurship Development : India's Experience, Finance and Development, March, 1986.

Bhaunik T. K., Lopsided Industrial Growth–I and II, *Financial Express, April 6 and 7, 1987.*

Bishwanath Goldar and Vijaya Seth, Spatial Variations in the Rate of Industrial Growth in India, *Economic and Political Weekly, June 3, 1989.* pp. 1237–1250.

Bognar Jozef, Economic Policy and Planning in Developing Countries, Akadomiai Kidao, Budapest, pp. 295–296.

Bulletin, *Financing of Small-Scale Industries : A Profile*, Reserve Bank of India (April, 1980).

Chanery H.B. and Tayler L., Development Patterns among Countries Overtime, *Review of Economics and Statistics*, Nov. 1968, pp. 391–416.

Dayakar C., SSI's Role in Growth of Small Indsutries in Andhra Pradesh, *Laghu Udyog Samachar*, 1979 4(2–3), pp. 39–41 and 58.

Diwan R.K., Returns to Scale in Indian Industry—A Comment, *Indian Economic Journal* 15, 1968.

Diwan R.K. and Gujarati D.N., Employment and Productivity in Indian Industries, *Artha Vijnan*, October, 1968.

Ganapathy V., District Industries Centres—How they will Work, *Industrial India*, February, 1979, pp. 21–22.

Habib, Small-Scale Industries Means to Eradicate Untouchability, *Khadi Gramodyog* (June, 1975).

Jain L.C., Development of Decentralised Industries. A Review of Some Suggestions, *Economic and Political Weekly* (October, 1980).

Khader Ali Khan, Techniques of Promoting Self-Employment in Urban Area, National Seminar on Promotion of Self Employment, New Delhi, 10th November, 1981.

Morahtetz David, Employment Implications of Industrialisation in Developing Countries—A Survey, *Economic Journal*, September, 1974.

Mukherji, Mukherji, Employment-Oriented Industries and their Role in State Economics, National Seminar on Industrialisation of States in India with Focus on Andhra Pradesh, University of Hyderabad, Agu, 7–9, 1987.

Oza A.N., Integrated Entrepreneurship Development Programmes—The Indian Experience, *Economic and Political Weekly*, May, 28, 934–951.

Ojha P.D., Financing for Small-Scale Enterprises in India, *Reserve Bank of India Bulletin*, RBI, Bombay, November, 1982, pp. 934–951.

Pannalal, Growth of Small-Scale Units—Role of Entrepreneurial Attitudes, *Laghu Udyog Samachar*, 1983, pp. 11–12.

Pillai P., Scale and Efficiency of Small-Scale Industries in India, *Asian Economic Review*, Vol. 20, No. 1, April, 1978.

Parameswaran K.P., Some Problems of Small-Scale Ancillary Industries, *Productivity*, Vol. 20 No. 1 April, 1978.

Patil, S. M., Prospects for Small-Scale Indsutries during the Eighties, *Bank of India Bulletin*, March, 1980. pp. 25–30.

———, The Complentary Role of Small Industry in India, *Man and Development*, Vol. 2, No. 1, 1980, pp. 15–21.

Pradhan H. Prasad, Neglected Aspects of India's Development Planning, *Economic and Political Weekly*, July 15, 1989, pp. 1591–1595.

Pradhan H. Prasad, Neglected Aspects of India's Development Planning, *Economic and Political Weekly*, July 15, 1989, pp. 1591–1595.

Prasad Agarwal, Industrialisation through Small-Scale Sector, The *Journal of Commerce*, Vol. XXXI, Part–III, No. 116, September, 1978.

Prasad Bhagwan, On Strengthening District Industries Centres, SEDME, SIET Institute, Vol. IX, No. 3, September, 1982, pp. 175–182.

Prasad and Viswanath, Financing of Small-Scale Industries by Commercial Bank, *Khadi Gramodyog*, Vol. 20, No. 3, 1973, pp. 163–172.

Raghava Reddy G., Bank Finance for Village and Small Indsutries, Eastern Economist (March, 1981).

Rangacharya S. S., Employment Generation and Income Distribution through Village and Small Indsutry in India : An Analytical Study : *SEDME* (June, 1983).

Raghupathi T., District Industrial Potential Studies—A Review of Scope and Methodology, *SEDME*, SIET Institute, Vol. III, No. 2, June 1981, pp. 71–80.

Rajuladevi, Indsutrialisation Adds Key to Rural Development, *Kurukshetra*, December, 1984.

Ramachandran K., Mynamism in Industrial Location—Location Theory Revisited, *Keio Business Review*, Vol. 24, No. 3 Japan, Keio University, 1988.

Ramachandran K., Regional Incentives and Small Enterprise Location—Some International Lessons, *Decision*, Vol. 15, No. 1, Jan.–March, 1988 pp. 41–47.

Raman C.S., Small Industry Prospects in India, *Laghu Udyog Samachar*, Vol. 7, No. 3, 1982, pp. 11–12.

———, Alernatives to District Industries Centres, *SEDME*, SIET Institute, Vol. III, No. 2, June, 1981, pp. 71–80.

Rangacharya S. S., Employment Generation and Income Distribution through Village and Smal lIndsutry in India : An Analytical Study : *SEDME* (June, 1983).

Rao S. L., Innovative Marketing Strategies : Small Enterprises Fight Large Established Companies, *Economic and Political Weekly*, August 26, 1989, pp. M. 127–M. 130.

Rao, V.K.R.V., Balance between Agriculture and Industry in Economic Development, *The Indian Economic Journal*, Vol. 34, No. 2, October–December, 1986, pp. 1–17.

Rondinelli Dennis, A., Small Indsutries in Rural Development : Assessment and Perspective, *Productivity*, Jan.-March, 1979.

Sandesara J.C., Employment in Indsutry : Seventh Plan Approach, *Economic and Political Weekly*, October, 20–27, 1984.

Sandesara J.C., Small-Scale Industrialisation—The Indian Experience, *Economic and Political Weekly*, March 26, 1988, pp. 240–654.

Shridharan L., Decentralisation and District Planning, *The Economic Times*, July, 24, 1986.

Shrivastava S.P., A Note on the District Industries, Centre Scheme, Indian *Journal of Economics*, Vol. LXVII April, 1987.

Smriti Mukherji, Employment-Oriented Industries and their Role in State Economics : 1981–82, Paper presented at the National Seminar on Industrialisation of Indian States, University of Hyderabad, 7–9, 1987.

Sathya Sundaram I., DIC at the Cross-Roads, *The Economic Times*, December 9, 1983.

Swaminathan M.C., Balanced Regional Development and Incentives for Industries, *SEDME*, SIET Institute, Vol. V, No. 3, December, 1978.

Tulpule Bagaram and R.C. Data, Rural Wages and Productivity in Industry—A Disaggregated Analysis, *Economic and Political Weekly*, Vol. XXIV No. 34, August 26, 1989, pp. M. 94–M. 102.

Varma R., Employment and Production in Small-Scale Industries : Some Findings of the RBI Survey, *Reserve Bank of India Occasional Papers*, 1980, pp. 155–166.

Vepa Ram K., DICs Play Effective Role in Industrialisation Sixth Plan in Retrospect, *Laghu Udyog Samachar*, Vol. X, No. 9, April, 1986, pp. 30–32.

Government of India, Ministry of Commerce and Industry

The International Planning Team : Report on Small-Scale Industries Estate, 1954.

National Small Industries Corporation (NSIC) : Okhla Industrial Estate, 1958.

Report of the Working Group on Industrial Co-operatives, 1958.

Rasma T.K., *Organised Industrial Districts—A Tool for Community Development*. U.S. Department of Commerce, Washington, 1954.

Ramakrishna K.T., *Finances for Small-Scale Industry in India*, Asia Publishing House, Bombay, 1963.

Ramanadhan V.V., *Economy of Andhra Pradesh*, Asia Publishing House.

Rao, Umamaheswara Ch., *Small-Scale Industries*, Popular Prakasam, Bombay, 1965.

Sandesra J.C., *Eficacy of Incentives for Small Industry*, Bombay School of Economics, 1980.

Sarma Ramakrishna, *Industrial Development of Andhra Pradesh*, Himalaya Publishing House, 1982.

Singh Baljit, *The Economics of Small-Scale Industries*, Satia Publishign Hosue, 1961.

Somasekhara N., *The Efficacy of Industrial Estates in India*, Vikas Publishing House, New Delhi, 1975.

Staley E., *The Role of Small and Medium Industry in Development*.

Staley E. and Morse R., *Modern Small Industry for Developing Countries*. McGraw Hill, New York, 1965.

Szita J., *Industrialisation in Economically Less-developed Countries*.

Thapper S.D., *Small-Scale Industry in India*.

Vasant Desai, *Organisation and Management of Small Scale Industries*, Himalaya Publishing House, 1983.

Report of the International Persepective Planning Team, 1963.

Development Commissioner (Small-Scale Industries), Report of 1968–69 and 1970–71.

Central Small Industries Organisation (SCIO) : Programme of Industrial Estates, Manubhai Shah.

Seventh Report of the Estimates Committee to Lok Sabha : Report on Small Scale Industies.

Development Commissioner (Small-Scale Industries), Industrial Estates, *Half Yearly Progress Reports.*

Small-Scale Industries Board, Report of the Sub-Committee on Industrial Estats.

Reports and Publications of Andhra Pradesh Government

dustrial Estates, Schemes for the Establishment of Assisted Industrial Estates, Department of Industries and Commerce.

ourth Five Year Plan, Andhra Pradesh, Draft Outline, Department of Planning and Co-operation.

ourth Five Year Plan—Outline and Programmes (1969–70 to 1973–74), Andhra Pradesh, Department of Planning and Co-operation.

ifth Five Year Plan, Andhra Pradesh Draft Outline, Department of Planning and Co-operation.

Fifth Plan, Andhra Pradesh, Approach, Technical Papers, Planning and Co-operation Department.

ifth Plan, Andhra Pradesh, Review of Development Technical Papers, Planning and Co-operation Department.

ixth Five Year Plan, Andhra Pradesh draft outline, Department of Planning Co-operation.

anning and Development of Backward Region, A Case Study of Rayalaseema Volume I, Planning and Co-operation Department, 1970.

rspective Plan for Rayalaseema Region, Andhra Pradesh, Vol. II, Plan Programmes, Planning and Co-operation Department, 1972.

rspective Plan for Rayalaseema Region, Andhra Pradesh, Vol. III, Methodology and detailed tables, Planning and Co-operation Department, 1974.

Director of Small-Scale Units in Andhra Pradesh, Volume I, Director of Industries.

Statistical Abstracts for the Years 1970–1984, Bureau of Economics and Statistics.

Annual Survey of Industries, Andhra Pradesh, Bureau of Economics and Statistics.

Report of the Annual Survey of Industries.

Annual Reports and Memorandum and Articles

Annual Reports of Andhra Pradesh Industrial Infrastructure Corporation (APIIC) from 1973–74 to 1984–85.

Memorandum of Association of Andhra Pradesh Industrial Infrastructure Corporation, 1974.

Brochure on land Acquisition, Andhra Pradesh Industrial Infrastructure Corporation Ltd.

Note on Activities of APPIIC.

Andhra Pradesh Industrial Infrastructure—A Catalyst for Industrial Growth in Andhra Pradesh.

Annual Reports of Andhra Pradesh Indsutrial Development Corporation (APIDC) Limited 1976–77 to 1983–84.

APIDC, New Dimensions in Development, APIDC.

Annual Reports of Andhra Pradesh State Small-Scale Industrial Development Corporation (APSSIDC) from 1976–77 to 1983–84.

Annual Reports of Andhra Pradesh State Financial Corporation from 1976–77 to 1983–84.

Annual Reports of Industrial Development Bank of India, 1981–82, 1982–83.

A compendium of APSSIDC services, Andhra Pradesh Small-Scale Industrial Development Corporation.

Other Reports

Government of Madras, Department of Industries and Commerce, All India Seminar on Indsutrial Estates, Reports on Proceedings, 1960.

Government of India, Small Scale Indsutries Board, Report of the Sub-Committee on Industrial Estates, 1960.

Study Group on Industrial Estates in Maharashtra, Bombay, 1966, p. 31.

Delhi Administration, Directorate of Industries, Okhla Industrial Estate, New Delhi, 1969, p. 149.

Survey of Backward Districts of Andhra Pradesh National Council for Applied Economic Research (NCAER) New Delhi, 1970.

Techno Economic Surveys of the States of India, NCAER.

A study of regional for the Fourth Plan, NCAER.

Report on IDBI assisted Industrial Estates in Karnataka and Andhra Pradesh, Industrial Development Bank of India, 1980.

All India Report on the Census of Small Units, Development Commissioner, Small-Scale Indsutries.

Industrial Policy, Administrative Staff College of India (A Course of Studies paper).

Industrial Potential Survey of Andhra Pradesh—Report of a Study Team—Sponsored by the IDBI–RBI, IFCI and APSFC.

Industrial Development of Backward Areas, Industrial Development Bank of India.

Index